Tears in Tehran

"Advance of the Caliphate "

Jon **Grainge**

Jon Grainge's
Tears in Tehran
"Advance of the Caliphate "

Jon Grainge

Born in the western suburbs of London Jon
saw service as a trainee RAF 'Jet Jockey'
before running his own Marine Sales business
for many years. Following a spell in Hotel
Sales and Marketing and Spanish property
sales he diverted his efforts into writing
adventure novels and photo-books under the
"European Photo-Book" collection

This book is a work of **complete fiction** albeit that is is partly based on the ongoing political events of 2014/15.
None of the characters are real and are the product of the author's rather vivid imagination. Any resemblance to actual people, either living or dead, is entirely coincidental. No fear or favour is shown to any particular country, person or group that may presently exist.

Tears in Tehran
"Advance of the Caliphate"

is a title from the
"European Photo-Book"
collection

www.blurb.com/user/store/hightrainman
www.amazon.com (search Jon Grainge)

———————————————

other **Novel titles** in the collection include:

"Taken from the Dunes"
"A Voice from Heaven"
"Fateful Decision"
"Appointment in Cairo"
"Appointment in Douz"
"Counter-Strike"
"Echoes from a Silent Enemy"
"Appointment in Puerto Banus"

___Dedication___

I dedicate this book to those innocent
souls who have so savagely perished in
their pursuit of helping those afflicted in
the recent Middle-East crisis of 2014/15

Jon Grainge

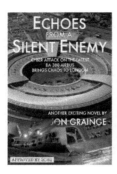

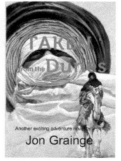

The "European Photo-Book" collection of NOVELS

___Preface___

This story is set in the region of Iraq, Syria and the
Islamic Republic of IRAN.

On hearing of the oppression in Syria a radical greengrocer from Pakistan decided to embark upon his formation of a new Caliphate in the Middle-East extending into Iran.
Does he succeed?

2015

Map of Iran

"Tears in Tehran"

Main Characters:

President of Syria:	President Almasi
IC Leader: (Islamic Caliphate)	Al-Malouf (Khalid Hesbari)
IC no.2: (Islamic Caliphate)	Homayoon Darshinika
Syrian leader:	Mohammed Hassan
IC tank commander:	Tariq Gajari
Syrian Militant leader:	Mohammed Hassan
Iranian dissident:	Yadullah Pisinah
President of Iran:	President Akbari
President of USA:	President Dick O'Shea
Joint Chief of US Staff:	General Atocha
Prime Minister of Israel:	Jacob Benayoun

Chapter One

It was as the deep Iranian sun rose gracefully above the jagged horizon that the amount of devastation to the ancient sacred city of Tehran could clearly be made out. The once thriving Golbon street, just south of the famed Azadi Arch Tower, which was normally alive with the bustling of hundreds of people and cars as they carried out their daily routines, was this day ...somewhat different.

It had started!

Amid the dust and debris the beautiful young Shahla Ushtra stood, covered from head to foot in her pure black but shredded burqa with tears, so many tears pouring down her palid cheeks from those deep brown Persian eyes, as she could only now fully observe and take in the hell and carnage caused from the day's actions. Her state of shock was only too apparent as the virtually naked dead body of her four year old daughter, Haleh, lay at her feet with no immediate reaction being outwardly displayed by Shahla. Her natural emotional concern for her only child had been inwardly suppressed to the point of Shahla not realising the enormity of the havoc and devastation thrown upon Tehran that day from the surprised attack.

It had been the policy of the ruling Assembly of the 290 Parliamentary Experts, as backed by President Akbari, that little of what had been developing in Iraq and Syria was to be told to the general populous of the Republic. They felt that a suppression of the facts would contain any sense of panic they might prevail should the full facts be known. The National internet system had been closed down following the attempted removal of atomic material from Qom by Al-Malouf some one week earlier. The military on the other hand had been sworn to secrecy to what they might have assimilated from hearsay within the ranks.

Smoke still headed gently skyward from so many burnt out buildings and vehicles leaving a greyish, blueish hue hanging ominously over the city, the Mosque in nearby Dehqan St was not now distinguishable as a building, water was gushing from several breakages in the water main and producing a river flowing towards the main Azadi autoway but it was the quantity of bodies lying so motionlessly dormant in the road or hanging unceremoniously from various levels of remaining buildings that shook Shahla to her core.

With no other apparent human movement within her sightline it led her to believe that she alone was the sole survivor in the Golbon area of Tehran.

Suddenly there was a bark. At least Shahla had the company of a local pet.

Several long minutes passed before Shahla regained her sense of reality and realisation of what had happened to her beautiful city that day. Her inner feelings began to thaw as gradually her head lowered as she saw the half buried torn body of Haleh lying prostrate at her feet. Struggling to clear the debris, brick by brick, Shahla eventually exposed the full remains of her only child before lifting her in her arms and implanting a long last kiss on her daughter's bleeding face. There was no point in looking for her husband, Darya, as four months earlier he had been called to serve his Artesh (military conscription service) and was presently based in the south of Iran at Bander Abbas on the Persian Gulf.

In realisation that there was nothing of her house or possessions left amongst the rubble and debris she stood on, the empty young Shahla wandered aimlessly down Golborn towards Azadi.

On reaching Tehran's most important street she suddenly found many thousands of people drifting towards the Tower. Not a vehicle was to be seen, just thousands and thousands of people all heading in one direction. Shahla joined in with the throng. Few words were being exchanged between the masses. The shock of what had happened extended across the whole city.

With the Tower clearly in sight Shahla was forced to halt her progress as the crowd was too dense for her to proceed any further. She could see that many of the buildings on both sides of Azadi had been either destroyed or badly damaged. It appeared to her that the area of her home around Golbon and Dehqan had received the most intense bombardment. As more and more people gathered around the massive fifty thousand square metre park the eerie silence was suddenly broken with the outburst of a verse from the Kur'an from a loud speaker emanating from the great Tower itself.

Following the short Islamic reading, the Imam introduced himself and whilst acknowledging the situation showing sympathy for the afflicted, called for calm and reflection. This only served to antagonise the audience who instinctively reacted with threatening chants which grew louder and louder as the crowd furthest from the Tower joined in the anger now spreading amongst the confused civilian population.

It did not take long for the anger to turn from a controlled shouting to the occasional shot being fired into the air. This heightened the mood even more and like a herd of sheep following the shepherd's instructions more and more guns were fired in anger and frustration.

Soon the estimated gathering of five hundred thousand or so had been moved toward a violent solution.

A grenade exploded at the base of the Tower killing all those in the immediate vicinity, then another and another which, having been thrown with great accuracy, landed at the feet of the Imam blowing him to pieces as it exploded.

The huge gathering, that had by now filled the entire length of Azadi from the Tower itself to Eslami Av and spilling into the main shopping street of Valiasr, went wild with a contagious rage.

The less scrupulous in the crowd took to looting from shops and private houses which further led to street fighting.

Once again the loud speaker issued a volume: it was that of Yadullah Pisinah.

A middle-aged radical with many connections outside of Iran and who was well aware of the development of the Caliphate activities in the next country. Being with the first group of protesters to arrive at the Tower and who threw the second of the grenades, had taken possession of the microphone for his address to the crowd.

Leaving no detail out Pisinah proceeded to inform the audience of the political situation and of the suppression of the information. He called for action from Akbari to face-up to the onslaught and bury the hatchet with America and call for their immediate help.

This drove the crowd wild who further displayed their agreement with Pisinah with ever increasing chants of

"Kill Malouf, kill Malouf, kill Malouf and down with Akbari"

How was such a riot to be contained?

Akbari, seated nervously in the luxury of his Green House, adjacent to the Sa'dabad Palace, had his lines of communication and was being kept fully informed of the development in the nearby streets.

He had no choice than to call out the army to qwell the riot but then with a second thought decided against this action. Half a million people and possibly growing to around a million, to control could prove to be an impossible task. What's more he might enlist the cooperation of this Yadullah Pisinah to direct his people's anger toward the Caliphate and away from himself.

These were desperate times for Iran and a possible turning point in it's illustrious history.

Wasting no time he issued a Presidential order for Pisinah to be brought to the Green House as soon and as quietly as possible. There was no need to inflame the situation more than was necessary.

With the city in turmoil and many of the buildings either destroyed or in a state of ruin with bodies strewn in many quarters,

Tehran was in a position of near revolution. The time for retaliatory action by Iran was at hand. Akbari must prepare his country for an all out war against the Caliphate with utmost haste.

How could this normally quiescent capital of the Islamic Republic of Iran have come to this?

Chapter Two

The involvement of Iran in the Middle-Eastern political struggle started just four weeks earlier, however the building of the Caliphate, which was to involve the commitment of so many countries from around the world, started many, many months before that.

As Syria's civil war fell slowly but surely into a bloodbath with several hundred thousand of it's citizens having been slaughtered by the

actions of it's President Almasi. The reluctance of the Governments of the United States and United Kingdom to militarily intervene in an attempt to curb the barbaric murder of innocent Syrian civilians allowed the build up of foreign, usually terroristic sympathisers from such organisations as
Al-Qaeda and Taliban, to assemble in Syria to outwardly defend the oppressed civilians in their vain attempt to overthrow President Almasi.
This build up of these incoming sympathisers from Afghanistan, Pakistan, Iraq, Mali, and several European countries continued unabated for month after month before the European and American Governments fully realised what was really happening right under their noses. They, plus the CIA and MI6, seemed totally unaware of the master plan being developed by a little known man from the back streets of Pakistan who had successfully infiltrated his presence into Allepo from Lahore. His long and arduous journey across the mountains and plains of Afghanistan, took him across the southern Iranian Desert and up the Persian Gulf to Iraq. From there, he and his small but dedicated team of one hundred or so followers who had escorted him, silently

enlisted the cooperation of a small army of disillusioned Sunni Iraqi extremists who then all made their way to Aleppo in Northern Syria.

This man, when he left Lahore was called Khalid Hesbari. Originally a greengrocer serving in his father's store in the slum area of Lahore, Hesbari developed an interest in politics and the sharing of power when his brother was killed by an American drone attack on the Afghanistan border. His growing sense of hate toward the west grew and grew as he sought out more information about the Islamic struggle with the West.

This inner hate rapidly turned to a severe hatred against all those who did not agree with his branch of Islam..he was Sunni. This hatred grew to such an extent that the alternative branch of Islam, Sheer, deserved a similar level of hatred in his eyes. They too were now about to become his sworn enemy.

This inner passion for the rise of the Sunni become so all encompassing to Hesbari that he actively enlisted several of his close family and friends to form a radical group which he called Al-Azaadi.

Hesbari spent the next year actively recruiting fellow Sunni Pakistani's to join Al-Azaadi. His numbers swelled to a few hundred. Having persuaded so many into this radical organisation, came then the problem of holding it together with a common purpose. It was all very well to talk the talk but several of the group were wanting to walk the walk! Action was required but against who? Within Pakistan itself there appeared very little appetite for an internal struggle so Hesbari fermented the idea of talking his revolutional and radical ideas to another country...........Syria!

Syria offered the perfect recipe within which he and his Al-Azaadi organisation could integrate and manipulate his hotbed ideas of Islam into the repressed civilian population. Not all of his followers were so keen on leaving their families to journey to such a far off land, possibly never to return, but nevertheless Hesbari had amassed a dedicated core of around one hundred who would join his crusade in Syria.

It was not without good reason that upon arriving on Syrian soil that the name of Hesbari and Al-Azaad, both of which came from an Urdu derivation, would be unknown, unrecognised and a possible barrier to the expansion of his ideas. To that end he changed his personal name to Al-Malouf and that of his organisation to IC. The initials of IC were thoughtfully adopted by Al-Malouf as they stood for his ultimate vision for Islam:

..Islamic Caliphate

At this early stage of his founding organisation the excited and radical Al-Malouf was not keen to expose his full intentions to those outside his very close circle so by the use of the initials instead of it's full title might not be so intimidating to new Syrian born members that he was about to actively recruit into the IC.

Having safely and covertly arrived in war torn Allepo Al-Malouf took little time to establish contact with a little known local Syrian militia and persuaded them to accept the help of his group in exchange to supplying his IC with a selection of weaponry and a place to live.

Al-Jabri Square was a semi-destroyed region of the city that had received thousands of shell hits from Almasi's Army and Air Force leaving very little trace of any buildings in tact. On entering the Square with the militia leader at his side and his men following close behind Al-Malouf could not believe the level of destruction. The smell of death hung heavy in the air,

"This will be your accommodation in here" pointed out Mohammad Hassan, better known as the 'Butcher' within his small band of rebels, as he led the way through the remnants of a front door, down a set of concrete steps and into a dark and depressing windowless collection of adjoining cellars. Just as the last of the men stepped through the doorway a high pitched aerial screaming noise could clearly be heard above their heads followed by a tremendous explosion on the other side of the street resulting in the building collapsing into a pile of bricks and a cloud of dust,

"Just another one of Almasi's tank shells. Nothing to worry about" commented Hassan *"you'll get used to that. We get a barrage of them every hour or so."*

Not wishing to show his utter revulsion at the disgusting conditions that he had led his followers to, all the way from the relative comfort of Lahore, Al-Malouf thanked his host for the facility and further requested the availability of some food.

"Food! There is no food in Hotel Allepo!. You will have to go out and about and scavenge whatever you can find from bins, empty

houses and thieving from those better off than us" replied The Butcher.

Just then another shell exploded in the street showering debris into the open doorway, down the steps and onto the shoulders of the somewhat perplexed group of Pakistani and Iraqi radicals.

"By the love of God what are we all doing here !" shouted one of the group trying desperately to withhold his growing inward fear.

Hesbari (Al-Malouf) realised that at this low communal ebb he now needed to get a grip of his men and hold them together if his dream for a new state of Islam is to continue. Brushing the dust from his clothes he decided to convene his first formal IC meeting in Syria. With Hassan clear of the property and well out of hearing range Khalid Hesbari stood on a nearby box and called the group to order in his usual commanding Urdu,

" My loyal friends. We are now here in Syria having travelled across several countries and it is now time to embark on our primary mission to support the militant Sunni cause. As from this point we will be known as IC (Islamic Caliphate) and I will be referred to as Al-Malouf. We will work

alongside Hassan's group for the time being as we recruit as many more members as possible. As you can see the living conditions here in Allepo are appalling but let's bear with it for the time being. The quicker we recruit more followers the quicker we can move forward and get out of this hell."

Following a stunned silence of several seconds with each man eyeing up the other next to him with the Iraqi contingent attempting to interpret what was being said, a communal clapping broke out followed by the raising of arms high in the air in support of their leader's vision.

All was ready.

The small but dedicated combined band of three hundred and fifty Pakistani's and Iraqi's were joined in their united passion to take on the world and construct their dream state.

Chapter Three

The next few weeks saw the IC fighting alongside the Syrian rebels, gaining valuable experience in hand to hand combat, strategic planning, familiarisation with an assortment of small and tactical weapons as well as establishing valued contacts within various radical factions also fighting in the Syrian theatre. The morale of IC grew and grew with Al-Malouf slowly gaining a reputation for his strong leadership and ability to obtain results. It was with a particular incident that occurred on 20th July in Al Jamaa Al Umawi steet that Al-Malouf gained his greatest step forward with his recruiting drive. He and several of his close group, including his second in command Homayoon Darshinika, were prospecting a possible target when out of the sun appeared a couple of Almasi's tanks catching Al-Malouf out in the open street. Without hesitation his group of twenty frantically broke for cover within the houses on each side of the street. The commander of the leading tank ordered the machine gun to open fire on the retreating rebels. Bullets flew at an alarming rate ricocheting off the road and buildings.

Quickly promulgating a plan to escape the inevitable consequence of when the T-72 released it's 125mm shells, Al-Malouf ordered his group to surrender and amass around the first tank with their hands held high in the air. Seconds after the tank commander raised his solid steel hatch and emerged from the tank's inners Al-Malouf swiftly reached for the revolver tucked in the rear of his trousers, aimed at the commander and fired three shoots in very quick succession. The commander fell from the turret onto the road. Two of the bullets had entered his skull killing him instantly. The machine gun operator only had time to unleash a five second volley as the spritely Pakistani rapidly leapt aboard the T-72 and dropped a grenade in through the open turret hatch. The soldiers inside stood no chance of survival.

At this point the machine gun of the second tank opened up upon the first hoping to hit the rebel atop their T-72. Al-Malouf with his dexterity managed to jump inside the charred tank before any bullets hit the steel. Meanwhile the remainder of the group hit the road and laid flat under the firing plane of the gun.

During IC's training programme with the Syrians the operation of a tank, especially the Russian built T-72, was on the curriculum so Al-Malouf was familiar with the firing procedure of the tank he was now sheltering in. Much of the instrumentation had been badly damaged by the grenade blast but due to the heavy Russian engineering the main barrel firing mechanism still seemed to be in working order. Heaving with great difficulty two of the body remains to the rear of the extremely cramped cabin Al-Malouf sat himself in the firing operator's chair and quickly established that the autoload system had already been selected leaving a round in the breech.

"Perfect" he shouted to himself as he rotated the T-72's turret through one hundred and eighty degrees to face directly at the other tank. Then having aligned the laser rangefinder pressed the firing trigger,

"Boom!" as the round left the barrel and hit the second T-72 clean on it's turret blowing the top half of the tank ten feet skyward.

Al-Malouf's men immediately leapt to their feet and jumped with joy in celebration of their salvation and victory.

Later that day Al-Malouf was heralded as a hero in front of the Syrians as he had now provided them with a usable Russian built tank which they could use against President Almasi.

The next couple of months saw the ranks of IC rapidly swell to several thousand which for the first time since the formation of the group included a hundred or so women.

Al-Malouf's popularity fast became a legend in Syria to the extent that he commanded more media lineage and television coverage, both on the local and International stage, than any of the rebel Syrian leaders themselves.

As Almasi's grip tightened on the weakening position of the rebels news of their demise attracted more and more International attention which in turn persuaded many hitherto latent Sunni pre-radicals from all corners on the Earth to up sticks and make their way to Syria to help in the cause.

What was causing more International media attention was the humanitarian plight of the one million refugees camping in nearby Lebanon, Jordan and Turkey. The Governments of most of the civilised world , the Charity agencies, such as the Red Cross and Medecins sans Frontiere plus The United Nations showed immense concern for the safety and future of the ever-growing tent cities developing in the Middle-East.

The rising global public opinion on the welfare of the refugees was diverting the attention of so many Governments away from the conflict itself and onto the numerical placement of the homeless civilians. With the global eye off-the-ball it allowed Al-Malouf to entrench himself further into the Syrian strongholds.

The death toll in the conflict climbed by some one thousand per week which eventually exerted so much pressure on the American, British and several European Governments to act; but still they resisted to intervene militarily.

The Turkish and Kurdish borders became the

flashpoints that initiated the turn in western policy.

As the summer of 2013 began to turn towards winter the now battle hardened and experienced Al-Malouf felt the time was right to embark on the next stage of his vision .. his eyes were firmly set on

Iraq!

Chapter Four

The last months embedded in the wrath of war engaged in the killing of other human beings and seeing friends die by savagery means had changed the character of khalid Hesbari beyond recognition.

His normal charm and friendly demeanour, gained from working in his father's grocery shop back in Lahore had perceptibly changed to that of a hardened criminal who would stop at nothing to achieve his aim. Even his physical appearance would now not be appreciated by his parents. The long black hair, the unshaven face, the two long scars on his left cheek, the bedraggled clothes and the lure he had now developed to fornicate with many women .. he had become intoxicated with his newly attained power.

However, this rugged, demanding character seemed to attract a massive influx of a nieve collection of bandits and hard radicals from many parts of the world. Like a moth to the light they came from Australia, Africa, Yemen, Afghanistan, Libya, UK and Algeria. These people were not so much interested in the rise of AL-Malouf's Islamic intentions but more to actively participate in criminal and violent actions without fear of being prosecuted by any authority. They came in their thousands giving Al-Malouf and his Senior Committee cause for concern as to how to handle them all.

It turned out that his natural, hitherto latent talent of sadistic leadership would qualify to be of a saving nature. Together with his newly learnt command of Arabic, Al-Malouf's Urdu and English placed him with an advantage over other Syrian commanders in the field. He had acquired total control over the foreign element flooding into Syria which the Syrian faction leaders could not either compete with or even communicate with..this gave Al-Malouf authority in Syria.

This had now become the time that NATO (North Atlantic Treaty Organisation set up in the late nineteen forties too deny the possibility of another major world conflict following the Second World War of 1939-1945) decided to take an interest in the activities of this new IC organisation.

The turning point which forced the Americans to call an emergency meeting of the Security Council of NATO came when

Al-Malouf led his a substantial contingent of his IC force across the Syrian border at Tall Kujik having passed close by to the Turkish border city of Al-Qamishli where several hundred more supporters joined the crusade to Iraq.

IC's strength had grown to nearly ten thousand in number and together with twenty five T-72's and hundreds of converted Toyota Hilux pick-up trucks each of which supported a single barrelled adaptation of the Russian built KPV 14.5mm anti-aircraft gun capable of an effective range of three thousand yards, represented a considerable threat to the stability of the whole region just at the time when it was acclimatising to self rule subsequent to the British and American withdrawal of forces following the 2003-2011 Iraq war.

With a full blown, lightly armed army behind him and encroaching towards the town of Mosul on the Iraqi/Kurdish border in north-west Iraq, Al-Malouf thought this the right time to declare his presence and intentions to his army but more importantly to the world.

Standing atop his leading T-72 as the convoy left the outskirts of AL-Qamishli he raised the ancient traditional black flag on which a paraphrase of the Shahada was quoted in white Arabic lettering,

"There is no god but God, Muhammad is the messenger of God."

Each and every one of the thousands of members of his IC following was then issued with a black head bandana and promptly informed that they would all be responsible for the formation of the

NEW CALIPHATE

with himself, Al-Malouf, as the elected Caliph or leader.

This Muslim state of political-Religious leadership was last seen in 1924 with the end of the Ottoman Caliphate. Those of a Sunni belief 'elect' their Caliph whilst those of Shia belief have theirs chosen by God.

With excitement of their new direction running through the ranks, thousands of AK-47 machine guns fired aimlessly into the evening air. The morale was now high enough for their first battle which was to be the taking of the major Iraqi city of Mosul. Situated four hundred miles to the north of Baghdad on the Tigris river it had an estimated population of one million so would represent a considerable challenge to capture but the prestige to the Islamic world of doing so would be enormous. With such a major city under his control Al-Malouf would then feel very confident in the establishment of his Caliphate.

The IC army with it's strength estimated at a little over ten thousand boldly set off in an extended convoy covering several miles in length, not wishing to provide an easy target for any stray Iraqi MIG aircraft who might attempt to stop them.

The journey across the north-western desert zone within the Neineva Province of Iraq took them via the compact Sinjar Mountain range where, upon hearing through the many social media sites, of the approaching IC army many thousands of completely innocent civilian Kurdish refugees from Mosul and it's surrounding area had decided to flee for safety.

On being informed of this flight of what he considered to be Kurdish Yazidi devil worshippers, Al-Malouf decided to temporary interrupt his advance on Mosul and totally eliminate those sheltering on the mountain in a savage way as an example to others. His strategy was to battle harden his latest recruits and also to put the fear of God into those still in Mosul before his forthcoming attack.

The advance up the northern slopes of IC's first wave of soldiers met with little opposition. The very lightly armed Yazidi men were no match for the barbarous activities of Al-Malouf's thugs who cut down the male men and boys without mercy but spared the women and girls for possible marriage potential for themselves. It had become IC policy to have as many children as possible by captured women to procreate the Caliphate for the future.

Word of this ongoing atrocity came to the ears of the CIA in Washington who had no choice than to pressurise President O'Shea into sanctioning airstrikes on the invading IC without even going back to the Security Council of NATO for an International consideration.

The American giant 'Gerald Ford' carrier with it's complement of fifty F-18 Super- Hornet fighter jets had, on orders from the

Pentagon, been patiently waiting in the Persian Gulf, some seventy five miles south west of Kuwait, for possible orders to intervene in the growing crisis.

The order to strike at IC in northern Iraq was received by Admiral Jones via Flash transmission at the late hour of 2005 hrs Zulu (local time) on October 12th.

At exactly 0015 hrs on the morning of the 13th in the dusk of a humid Arabian morning Captain 'hotshot' Zeegler plunged his two throttles fully forward and engaged both afterburners seconds before the catapult rocketed the F-18 from a standstill to one hundred and seventy knots in the space of three seconds. Within a further thirty seconds the heavily armed Super-Hornet was stabilised at his initial cruising altitude of twenty one thousand feet on a heading of three five zero degrees and at a speed of five hundred knots. At 0018 hrs the second F-18 took to the air followed at 0021 hrs by the third and final fighter jet.

It had been calculated by the powers that be in Washington that a first strike of three aircraft dropping the correct ordnance would be sufficient to demoralise the militant fighters of IC and encourage them to withdraw from Mount Sinjar. How wrong this decision would turn out to be!

In a 'V' formation thundering over Iraq at FL21 (flight level 21, twenty one thousand feet) the squadron was soon required to search out the three waiting KC-135 Stratotankers for a top-up of kerosene. The one thousand mile each way journey for the Super-Hornets would necessitate a couple of top ups to ensure a state of flight. Sure enough showing up on the Raytheon nose radar just south of Baghdad were the signatures of the three tankers holding in adjacent racetrack patterns.

With radio contact made the tankers extended their re-fuelling booms and the boom operators, sat in the rear control cabins prepared to receive their customers. Inch by inch the F-18's eased up to the wavering probe until their extended receiver arms made contact with the probe baskets. Four minutes of continual fuel flow was sufficient to satisfy the sixteen thousand five hundred pounds of fuel capacity of each F-18 which included the long range external tanks. Zeeglar and his colleagues then gently pulled back before opening their throttles and descending to five hundred feet above the Iraqi desert for their run to Mount Sinjar. This low level approach to the battlefield would avoid any possible SAM (surface to air missile) lock-ons should the IC be in possession of any captured Iraqi FN-6 Chinese built shoulder launchers that Iraq was known to have had in it's inventory.

Dawn was just breaking as Captain Zeegler received his latest intelligence of the whereabouts of the main IC force from the pair of Rivet Joint surveillance aircraft that had been circling at very high altitude above Mount Sinjar. Decision made: Captain Zeegler ordered the attack to begin with a rapid combined bomb drop on the main force and then a dash for home.

Caught totally by surprise Al-Malouf never saw the three F-18's release their combined total of twelve GBU Paveway 11 guided bombs which one after another exploded amongst his ranks just arousing from their night's slumber. The balls of fire rose high into the air lighting up the Iraqi mountain side for a brief time as the screams from hundreds of dying soldiers gradually depleted.

Having confirmed from his co-pilot/weapons officer the strike to have been successful all three aircraft applied the full thrust of their GE 414's with afterburners to vacate the area as swiftly as possible on a south easterly heading. However, as Zeegler's port engine wound up to almost one hundred percent power one of the blades in the aft turbine shattered sending several fragments of high tensile alloy into the rotating turbine. This rapidly resulted in an exhaust explosion at the rear of the engine which in turn sent debris into the starboard engine. Zeegler's instrument panel lit up like a Christmas tree with several warning klaxons filling the cockpit with mixture of differing noises.

The experienced Captain instinctively knew that the aircraft was finished and immediately ordered his co-pilot to eject shortly followed by his own evacuation.

During his slow descent at the end of his chute Zeegler could easily make out in the yellowing dawn the welcoming party of terrorists eagerly waiting for him to fall into their arms. The Captain was fully aware of the possible consequences of being taken prisoner, so attempted to reach into his flightsuit breast pocket for his 'happy-pill' but was frustratingly prevented from doing so due to the pressure of the parachute strap exerted over the velcro fastening. His co-pilot had no such difficulty and was dead upon making contact with the ground.

Al-Malouf was pleased with his captive which

upon examination of Zeegler's dogtags served to confirm that America was now involved and presumably fully committed to his war. A rye and satisfied smile appeared across Al-Malouf's face. He had drawn the United States back into Iraq only a couple of years after they vacated vowing never to return.

It was not for a hour before the self appointed Caliph of IC was informed of the demise of his second in command and very , very dear friend from Lahore, Homayoon Darshinika. His charred body was recovered from his tent and laid before Al-Malouf. The distress on his face was clear for all to see. He had known Homayoon for fifteen years. They had been at school in Lahore together. It was he (Al-Malouf) who had persuaded him to embark on this Caliphate re-incarnation and stood now starring at his body. The anger within grew,

"Bring me the American pilot who I hold fully responsible for the death of my good friend!" he ordered. This opportunity delivered to him by God he saw as a chance to ease his plunder of Mosul.

Zeegler was duly thrown to the ground in a cloud of morning dust with the boot of a trusted soldier pressing hard across his neck.

"You come here to kill my people now I will

send a message to your people. Give me your scimitar and get a video camera and someone who can operate it" he shouted at one of his soldiers in a fit of anger.

With the American pilot on his knees and head forced into a bowing position Al-Malouf turned to the tiny ipad camera,

" President O'Shea. You send your airmen to destroy me and my Caliphate. You will not succeed. You have raised my profile in this attempted act and greater increased my resolve to capture the city of Mosul. For those in Mosul who resist my progress and do not convert to Sunni beliefs and deny my Caliphate what is about to happen to the American will be imposed on you!" and swiftly brought the razor sharp scimitar down onto Zeegler's neck. His head rolled away down the shallow hill in amongst the soldiers. The camera was directed toward the prostrate torso lying in a pool of blood gently draining into the sand.

"Put that video onto youtube now so that the world can see" ordered Al-Malouf as he raised both his arms to command everyone's full attention.

"We will leave these Yazidi's to the fate of nature on this barren rock. We march this minute onward to Mosul."

Chapter Five

All hell broke loose as the video got picked up and shared across the internet. World condemnation of it's content could not be suppressed. The Security Council again met, the British and American Governments arranged to meet for private consultations, the Iraqi Government shook with fear and the world's media had a heyday analysing possible repercussions. The mood in Mosul was one of fear. Thousands fled either south east to the Kurdistani city of Irbil or north to the Turkish border. This presented an enormous humanitarian headache for the Charitable services even before IC had sight of Mosul.

The airstrikes from the Gerald Ford carrier relentlessly continued on the progressing IC

army, however, with little effect as
Al-Malouf's so called Generals recommended
that their hoard of relatively undisciplined
soldiers be spread thinly over a wide area and
only travel at night during their two day
march to Mosul.

Taking full advantage of the low winter sun
dropping tenderly behind his lines Al-Malouf
finally threw his forces at the city on the
evening of the 16th. The T-72's spearheaded
the attack by taking the opportunity of a
quick strike driving down the M10 auto
expressway and the southerly entry road of Al
Mintaga As Sina'iyan Street.

Announcing their arrival by laying down a
barrage of 125 mm shells into the outer
western suburbs of the city, the Iraqi
defences, with the help of a nearby division of
Peshmerga soldiers from nearby Kurdistan,
returned fire with their similar

T-72's and several Abrams M1's supplied to
them by the Americans post the Iraq war
(2011). Neither side managed to apply any
degree of accuracy with their shots so little
damage was inflicted except for the
demolition of a few innocent houses.

The line of IC tanks moved steadily forward
closely followed by hundreds of Hilux
gunships and several thousand chanting foot

soldiers.

As the city development itself was reached Al-Malouf's generals ordered a fanning out of the Hilux pick-ups and to enter the city be any street, road, path or track they could find shooting anyone in their path. Planning had dictated that the tanks would be too busy contesting each other to interfere with the progress of the Hilux gunships festering in and around the suburbs of the city.

This simple but effective strategy worked. It worked well as unexpectedly to Al-Malouf the Iraqi soldiers, short on ammunition and low on morale especially having seen the youtube video, surrendered in their hundreds forcing the remaining Pershmerga to retreat back to Kurdistan. The sacking of the large city of Mosul took less than three hours to achieve! Al-Malouf could not have been in a more joyous but rather surprised mood. This victory had more than made up for the loss of his good friend, Homayoon.

Ordering all the captured Iraqi officers and several hundred enlisted men plus the heads of the Civil Administration to be brought to the well known Al-Mawsil Stadium on Bad Sinjar Street, Al -Malouf set about the end of the beginning of his master Caliphate plan. His soldiers roamed the streets all evening commanding all citizens to attend the forthcoming event at the Stadium the following morning at 1100 hrs.

The night of the 16th of October 2013 would pass in terror for the residents of Mosul as houses were burnt, shops looted and people shot in the streets by the invading IC. Dawn of the 17th, amid the burning and smouldering in much of the city ruins, saw queues of people being herded toward to Stadium from all directions to hear and see what spectacle Al-Malouf had in store for them. That morning's activity would be written in the annals of history.

At precisely 11am, with the warmish sun high above the nearby Zagros Mountains in nearby northern Iran, Al-Malouf dressed in a full black dishdasha, black bandana and carrying his adopted black standard, climbed onto the hastily constructed stage to join several of his leadership and a line of twenty five of his followers each holding a scimitar in their right hand.

He raised the microphone to his mouth,

"Mosul is now under the control of my IC and from this point is now the centre of my new Sunni Caliphate. I am now your Caliph Al-Malouf. Before you" pointing at the large collection of prisoners gathered in front of

the stage, " *are the old leaders of your forces and administration who are about to die. I offered them no choice but I do now offer you all a choice to either convert to my Caliphate as a Sunni Muslim or suffer the same fate.*"

Raising his hand the first twenty five prisoners were hauled onto the stage and commanded to kneel.

As each of the scimitars came down Shia blood ran across the stage. For one and a half hours this barbarous performance continued with the grass beneath the stage unable to absorb any more of the blood. The headless bodies mounted up behind the staging. It was finished, or so the crowd thought until their Caliph spoke once again,

"Your leaders have been cleansed, now I give you your chance. Who amongst you will NOT join me and convert?"

At first there was near silence until one in the crowd shouted abuse at Al-Malouf, then another and another and then several hundred. Encouraged by growing anger, the mood of the vast crowd of many, many thousands changed to rage and rapidly turned into a riot.

Al-Malouf's soldiers began to open fire and unleashed their AK-47 magazines with vigour.

The non-discriminating killing continued for half-an-hour before hands of submission began rising into the air. The shooting ceased. Al-Malouf took to the microphone again,
"Those who will not join me come forward" he shouted in a callous rage.
Like sheep to the slaughter those whose faith would not waiver stepped toward the stage.
The executions continued until afternoon. The carnage was disgusting. Men, women and children lay there. The horror was enough for the living remainder to jointly swear allegiance to the new Caliphate.
From that point the Caliphate had been born out of so much blood.

Mosul lay quiet, very quiet.

Once the CIA, United Nations and eventually the world press heard of this atrocity, global opinions and condemnations began to be continually voiced.
The result of that day's actions had polarised the world into two views:

those with and those against
The Caliphate.

The time of mere protestation on the progress of the IC had passed; action, real action was now demanded by the public the world over.

Without requiring too much persuasion the world decided to jointly respond and so formulated a plan for several countries to coordinate air strikes . A 'boots on the ground' campaign was ruled out at this stage as few countries were willing to commit such substantial resources however were wishing to keep an open mind on the future after appraising the effectiveness of the forthcoming air strikes.

Within a week of much international diplomatic activity a strike force of some one hundred fighter aircraft from the United States, United Kingdom, Australia, Canada and France had amassed in several bases which included Cyprus, UAE , Kuwait and two aircraft carriers moored in the Persian Gulf. Carefully each Air Force coordinated it's own activity schedules with the others and began operations over Mosul. The French concentrated on rendering the airport runway useless for any possible IC usage whilst the Canadians took out the transport infrastructure such as roads, rail lines and kept an eye on any river traffic. The rest of the coalition simply flew around seeking out and destroying presentable targets such as moving vehicles, groups of soldiers or tanks etc.

It took Al-Malouf a couple of weeks entrenched in Mosul to check-out his captured equipment and to assess the quality and quantity of his new 'devoted' followers. He was pleased with what he saw as his arsenal had swollen by a dozen Abrams and twenty T-72 tanks, several D30 Howitzer field guns, a multitude of M240 and DShK heavy machine guns, a couple of tracked APC's and simply hundreds of hand held machine guns. Then to top his shopping list were the contents of several looted banks which proved too much for his men to count precisely but they estimated at around fifty million dollars US.

Together with the revenue from several of his captured oil wells back in Syria plus offerings from a few sympathetic middle-eastern countries, Al Malouf's coffers were overflowing. This would allow him to purchase more military equipment and pay all his followers a 'salary' making IC the richest and most generous terrorist group in history.

The persistent bombing by the coalition had very minimal impact on the confident
Al-Malouf who spent most of his time enthusiastically purveying his equipment in the relative security within the city precincts and allocating its role in the next stage of his master plan. Parades were held. Promotion within his ranks of officers concluded and the all-black uniform issued to all new active recruits.

Time to relax before embarking on his next exploit., however, it was at this time after being in the field and under such pressure for such a long time that a sudden desire of female company swept over him. No doubt the continual sight of fornication amongst his men played heavily on his sub-conscience implanting the idea of him joining in the celebrations and implementing his own orders.

The task of finding a selection of suitable candidates to satisfy his carnal urge was delivered to one of his 'converted' junior Iraqi officers who eluded to know where to find acceptable stock!

The following morning having been disturbed from his deep slumber in the Presidential suite of the Hotel Mosul by a nearby explosion delivered by a British

Tornado jet, the Caliph arose. Then following a hearty breakfast was presented with a line-up of six of the most beautiful girls, ranging in age from fifteen to twenty two, that his new lieutenant could obtain.

Never before had the greengrocer from Lahore been subjected to such temptation. The usually decisive Pakistani was completely spoilt for choice so fell to the only solution available to him and took the lot :

the Caliph's harim.

They would escort him throughout the rest of his campaign on which he was about to embark.

Chapter Six

With his senior advisers comfortably sat on the three sofas in the reception foyer of the hotel AL-Malouf sought their advice for the taking of his next prize which he considered to be the big one...

Baghdad

Several strategies were presented but the one that Al-Malouf favoured above all the others was that offered by his Syrian colleague from Allepo, Yousef Al-Halbi. Nominated as a senior commander Al-Halbi dearly shared the vision of his leader and would similarly undertake any task to obtain the objective.
His suggestion was extreme and would almost certainly lead to the deaths of thousands, possibly hundreds of thousands of innocent lives in Baghdad but it presented

a high chance of being successful.

The plan included a double strategy both of which should be activated concurrently.

The first was to immediately contact known groups of dissidents, who sang to the tune of the growth of Sunni Islam, in the European cities of London, Amsterdam, Berlin and Paris and instruct them to cause as much havoc as possible in those cities, all of which to be carried out on a pre-determined date. This would serve to heavily occupy the world's media and twittersphere whilst the second strategy was being undertaken by IC in Iraq ...that of blowing up the huge dam on the entrance to the Tigris river at Lake Mosul.

Al-Halbi further advised that a fast moving force of some one hundred fully armed men aboard Hilux jeeps might reach the dam from Mosul in around three to four hours and could remain for the most undetected by coalition intelligence if they travelled by night in a stretched out single line convoy. Not expecting an immediate strike in the light of so much international media activity the protective force currently stationed at the dam would be unprepared and be easily overcome by the IC force. Allowing a couple of days would be sufficient for the dam to be wired up and fully prepared for detonation. With the dam eventually breached the anticipated fifty foot high tidal wave would travel down the Tigris and through the heart of Baghdad itself before finally dispersing in the Persian Gulf.

The shock of a fifty foot tsunami wave hitting their city would destroy a great deal of Baghdad but more importantly further devastate the local population.

Whilst the strike force was making it's way to the dam Al-Halbi suggested the IC army move out of Mosul, as this city would also suffer the effects of the wave, and split into two divisions. One division containing the tanks and five thousand men travel toward Baghdad via the relatively open desert away from the Tigris whilst the second division of twenty thousand plus men and light Howitzers travel through the mountains via Karkuk. By splitting into two Al-Halbi thought this might help to wrong-foot and confuse the coalition air forces who would be continually attacking from the air. The closeness of the second division, with Al-Malouf himself at it's head, to the Iranian border and traversing mountainous terrain might also help to protect them from marauding coalition pilots.

With the city fervently attempting to recover from the receding waters of the Tigris both divisions would make their advance into the chaos of Baghdad from differing directions.

This plan having been heard in all its detail by Al-Malouf's assembled advisers was then offered for their comment and final approval albeit that Al-Malouf had already made up his mind to put this plan into operation within days.

That approval came unanimously.

Five thousand miles away in the placitude of the Pentagon on the banks of the Potomac in Washington the defence chiefs were busily engaged in studying the aerial photographs of the last few days of bombing on Mosul and the surrounding area. The ineffectiveness of the bombing was clear to be seen with potholes littering the desert floor and only the occasional burnt-out vehicle visible. The severely limited strikes on the city itself, ordered for humanitarian reasons, had caused damage but very small in nature. The frustration endured by the coalition pilots had been well documented and forwarded to their commands.

There was a knock on the Defence Secretary's door and in entered a female member of staff,

"Sir I have the latest intel from the Gerald Ford" she spoke in a positive voice handing the file to the Secretary of Defence.

On close inspection of the aerial images of Mosul an area of interest aroused General Midwinter's attention and requested the image be brought up on the giant Reece screen,

"There Mr Secretary. Do you see the objects gathering in the south-eastern suburbs of the city."

All eyes were focused on the slightly pixelated image.

"Tanks! Those are tanks Sir!" shouted Joint Chief of Staff General Atocha.

"Very well Gentlemen order one of the Rivet Joints to obtain more images ASAP" ordered the Defence Secretary.

Night fell in northern Iraq which saw the small convoy of twenty five Hilux pick-up's slowly merge in with the general traffic on the M5 autoroute heading in the northerly direction whilst in the south-east of Mosul the main IC army of twenty-five thousand men began its exit out of the city on the 80 highway.

The tanks led the mighty column at their

maximum speed as the combined force had to use the highway to cross the Tigress tributary some twenty miles from Mosul before splitting into two forces. Al-Malouf fully realised that the patrolling American spy planes would pick up their movement so wanted to minimise the time his force would take to reach the river. It would take several hours for the complete army to cover this vulnerable distance but it was within

Al-Malouf's plan for the coalition to observe the mass movement thus lessening the possibility of his dam strike force being spotted.

The latest infra-red images were presented to the waiting Secretary of Defence who immediately threw it onto the screen.

"I knew it, tanks and a complete army Sir on the move south" shouted General Atocha. All those gathered had no doubt of what they saw and the conclusion they drew ...

Baghdad had to be the target.

"Get onto the Chief of the Armed Forces in Baghdad and warn them of a possible attack" the Defence Secretary requested of Atocha and realising then the impossibility of any coalition aircraft being able to reach the area in time,

" and tell them to get some of their SU-24's into the air and take out the bridge over the Tigress with utmost speed then order Admiral Jones to strike the column at first light" he continued.

The cool night air felt good blowing into Al-Malouf's face as he stood erect aboard his T-72 as it sped down the highway touching nearly twenty miles per hour. He had to get his complete army across the bridge before the coalition could muster an air strike to destroy it. Time was of the essence.

Then out of the gloom appeared the near tower of the bridge. Within a couple of minutes the Russian T-72 had crossed safely.One after the other the tanks traversed the Tigress and when on the eastern bank continued to set up a line of fire in a westerly direction in anticipation of any coalition aircraft attempting to strike the bridge. The progress of the militant force across the bridge continued unopposed for a couple of hours. It was as the last of the stragglers approached that out of the brightening sky came three low level high speed jets which between them released six air to ground rockets several of which detonated on making contact with the tarmac surface of the bridge. An estimated two hundred and fifty Jihadists perished in the bridge's destruction.

Al-Malouf immediately ordered his tanks to open fire but it was one of the shoulder held APGs that caught the Iraqi SU-24 in the tail sending it and it's pilot to eternity.

The remaining two Russian made jets on seeing their colleague's demise swiftly flew round for a one off strafe of gun fire from their 23mm cannon. Each unleashed their full payload of five hundred rounds on

Al-Malouf's massive Hilux convoy destroying at least twenty trucks and their occupants before returning to base in Baghdad.

Observing the many trails of rising black smoke sat atop his vantage point on a small rise, Al-Malouf now realised his drive towards Iraqs capital was firmly on the coalition's radar. His one hope was that the other column heading towards the dam had remained undiscovered.

Leaving his dead followers to suffer from natural decomposition and with no time to loose Al-Malouf ordered the planned split of his army. The tank division accompanied by five thousand Jihadists panned out into a wide formation across the desert floor and headed in a southerly direction. The rest of the force accelerated east towards the foothills of the Zagros Mountains just skirting the Kurdish town of Irbil.

Progress was good as dawn light climbed from the horizon.

The clear image of the two armies pressing on toward Baghdad became of grave concern to the Defence Secretary as he stood and observed the latest intel from his Rivet Joint surveillance aircraft. It became obvious to the Chief of Staff, stood next to the Secretary, that the northern column was using the closeness to the mountainous Iranian border both as a physical and Political shield as it would possibly entail coalition aircraft entering Iranian airspace to be able to attack. This would take time to organise with the Iranians in Tehran..time they did not have!

The tank advance on the other hand would present no problem so suggested to the Defence Secretary that all coalition aircraft concentrate on taking out the fifty or so tanks whilst he made diplomatic approaches to President Akbari.

Darkness was beginning to fall as the convoy turned off the highway and took to the numerous desert tracks that led to the dam. The convoy leader had decided on a full head on approach with all vehicles involved. This 'all or nothing' attack caught those on gate duty completely by surprise and were hastily overrun without offering any resistance of consequence. All was going well. By the time the sleeping defence force in the No. 2 barracks had been stirred the IC soldiers burst through the wooden door and cut them to pieces. Within the space of ten minutes the dam had been taken! Oh how easy that was!

Chapter Seven

The day drew on as Al-Malouf made progress through the foothills. The occasional attack upon his column from small groups of Peshmerga troops from Irbil had little effect. With the binoculars held tight to his eyes the air attacks on his tanks could clearly be made out down on the plains. They were being subjected to severe punishment and taking losses so Al-Malouf thought this time to call the sacrificial groups he sent to the major cites. Whether or not his communication was about to be picked up by coalition surveillance mattered not to the Pakistani greengrocer as he dialled in the first mobile number.

Within the hour sporadic and totally unplanned attacks on innocent civilians in main line railway stations took place in Amsterdam, Paris, London and Berlin. Bursts of AK-47 rounds were unabatedly unleashed amongst the travellers in

St. Pancras, Gare du Nord, Amsterdam Centraal and Hauptbahnhof stations sending hundreds to their death before the city Police attended the scene and eventually cut the terrorists down.

The world's media, the internet and the twittersphere lit up with the headlines, millions took to the streets and police and military ordered to full alert through Europe ....exactly what Al-Malouf had wanted!

Any media emphasis that existed on his exploits in Iraq were immediately withdrawn but more to the point the coalition 'military eye was taken off the IC ball'.

Disgusted, appalled and shocked the public demonstrations throughout Europe grew and grew and grew. Millions took to the streets in peaceful protest calling for the military to intervene and bring to justice those responsible for this slaughterous carnage.

On seeing the unprecedented images on his satellite television President Akbari became very accepting of the Defence Secretary's requests but only to the point of offering Iranian air strikes and not authorisation of the use of American aircraft within his airspace. To a point, this satisfied the American President who then curtailed his call to concentrate on other matters of urgency.

The Iranian Air Base at Hamadan was duly contacted and ordered to scramble a squadron of ancient but serviceable F-4D fighter jets to bomb the IC column in the Zadros foothills.

The inaccuracy of the old analogue Iranian jets and limited capacity of their payload did little to impede Al-Malouf's progress. A few pick-up's destroyed and a few men killed or wounded was an acceptable loss to the Caliph. What had angered him though was the intervention of Iran... his hated enemy of Shia Muslims.

As night fell Al-Malouf halted all his forces for that day. The following day would be momentous and wished to hold a final brief with his leaders before the assault on Baghdad. They were now only a couple of hours from the northern suburbs of the city.

All through that night the Jihadi soldiers unloaded the tons of explosives from the rear of the Toyotas and carefully assessed the weakest point of the dam before strategically planting the boxes of HE (high explosive). With access gained to the network of internal passageways deep within the wall of the concrete dam the complete eastern section had been littered with the wooden crates of HE and all connected to a central igniter. All was ready. The commander texted Al-Malouf. At 0455 hrs Al-Malouf returned his message, *"Go!"*
The explosion of two and a half tons of HE could have been heard through the cool morning air twenty miles away. Very little could be seen though as the flames and smoke were well contained within the wall. At first following the detonation there was no movement. Had they failed? Maybe not

enough HE? But then spurts of water began to excrete from the main wall..then more until a waterfall fell to the river below. CRACK! The wall began to collapse. Another CRACK! and down it went allowing a mighty cascade of water to pour into the Tigress. With a billion tons of a fresh reservoir water behind it the resulting waterfall burst the river banks and quickly built up a tsunami wave which grew and grew in height as more water thundered into the river behind.

Mercifully as the fifty foot high wave raced into the city of Mosul most people were still asleep and never knew what hit them; as for the others, there was nowhere to hide, nothing they could do except.... pray.

Now laden with tons of urban debris including vehicles the wave embarked on its two hundred and seventy five mile journey to Baghdad. The sheer quantity of water stored in Lake Mosul still poured into the Tigris imposing even more kinetic energy into the wave which now rushed towards the towns of Tikrit and Samarra. These towns stood little chance to avoid total destruction.

With even more debis in it's clutch the wave now had a clear run to accelerate towards the capital.

The warning of the oncoming disaster conveyed to the Iraqi authorities by the Pentagon, who analysed the situation from their satellite imagery, gave no time for Baghdad to prepare. Many of the officials in possession of this message scrambled to pick up their families and drive out of the city into what they thought might be the safety of the countryside. They would be wrong.

At precisely 0923 hrs the massive wave struck the first suburb of Baghdad. on encountering the first major bend in the Tigress the wave proceeded straight on, both across the land and down the river course in a single extended wall of water.

The Al-Kadhimiya Mosque collapsed under the water pressure. The Madenat Alelem University disappeared. Still the wave continued. The Hospital fell, great sections of the 14th July Street were washed away, as was the Zoo but the worst came at Um Al-Khanazir Island where the river meandering was at it's laziest. There stood the main University, Al Jami'ah Street and two bridges all of which were reduced to rubble in the wave's wake. The resistance offered by the buildings of Baghdad eventually slowed the wave down to a walking pace as it exited the city boundary and continued on the full length of the Tigress through Basra and into the Shott Al Arab to disperse in the Persian Gulf.

The early morning scene in Baghdad was like that from a disaster movie. Virtually all of the city lay under ten feet of dirty, infected water with thousands of bodies floating on the surface, even the airport was submerged. The countryside for as far as the eye could see was completely flooded. It was a catastrophic scene.

Through his binoculars Al-Malouf could just make out the unfolding scene in the distance. Time to proceed as the few miles left to travel to meet up with the remains of his tank division would only take him a couple of hours.

Approaching the city limits brought into view the sheer devastation that his plan had imposed on this once ancient and fabled city. Had he gone too far? This thought continually ran through his mind.

The water level had subsided sufficiently for Al-Malouf's Jahadi followers to be shocked at what they saw as they entered Baghdad through what used to be streets and roads.

What was left of the population offered no resistance to IC's slow and difficult entry into the city. This was not the victory the man from Lahore wanted with so many dead. It would take years for this conquest to come back to what could be called meaningful life. Unlike Mosul there were precious few useful Shia Muslims to whom conversion might be offered.

A hollow victory it may have been but a victory nevertheless for the IC as Al-Malouf proclaimed it as the new capital of his Caliphate.

The shock and horror of what was happening in Europe and the Middle-East sent shivers of non belief down the backs of the American Administration and Council of the United Nations. The sacking of Baghdad would surely mean declaring an all out war against IC with hundreds of thousands of coalition 'boots on the ground' thought President O'Shea as he sat with his head in his hands in the Oval Office. An emergency meeting of the Security Council was convened for the following day.

As anticipated the showing of hands at the Councils meeting in New York for the immediate intervention with a united army of troops was unanimous. It was generally accepted that at least two weeks would be required to establish such an international force and for it to be assembled in southern Turkey.

Al-Malouf was at a loss as to where to start in the wreckage of Baghdad. The scene was apocalyptic. The mud soaked streets strewn with debris and bodies made it difficult to move about. Vehicles were piled up against water flow restrictions such as walls and buildings. Trees and bushes lay about. His new capital city was beginning to smell! How would history write this episode?

Having declared Baghdad as the new capital of the Caliphate was beginning to look non-productive and unattractive to the leader with so much ambition for his dreams of a Sunni Islamic State. Consultation with his leadership in Mosul using the dark side of the internet gave him no solace as the damage sustained to that city as well as Tikrit and Samarra was similar to that of Baghdad!

For sure the greengrocer had totally underestimated the fall-out from the destruction of Mosul Dam. Here he stood, with the majority of Iraq at his command, but what a country he had conquered ... a bomb site! The repair and renovation required to bring the country back into the civilised world was far beyond the capabilities of his meagre IC. To increase the pressure further the information he had gained from his hacking of the Pentagon's central computer clearly showed the build up of coalition forces both to the north and south of Baghdad in preparation for an immediate invasion of his self declared Caliphate.

It was obvious to Al-Malouf that at the point at which he now stood his Caliphate was doomed. It would only be a matter of time before his destruction would be complete.

His pacing up and down the waterlogged ruins of Saddam Hussein's old Presidential Palace in front of his leading officials, hour after hour with not a word being spoken throughout the building, started to send an air of despondency shimmering down the ranks of his followers. The looting slowed to a natural end. The raptures of a joyous victory had subsided. Even what few executions that were in progress began to loose public interest. A sense of 'what do we do next' floated around the city. A decision for the future direction of the new Caliphate was desperately needed if it was to hold together ...... and that decision had to be immediate!

As the evening sun drifted toward the desert ridge it came to him. Al-Malouf had formulated his plan - risky but what had he and his jihadists to loose.

Gathering the most senior and trusted of his Council together in the Great Hall he stood erect and confident on a nearby guilt table and proudly announced the plan,

"My dear friends and fellow Muslims. You have followed and assisted me in the formation of our New Caliphate. However there are other who would destroy this and beckon to the north and south. Soon the coalition army will be at our door so it is time to move forward to another place where our victory will be that much sweeter and our power that much greater.......

Tehran."

There was a sudden stirring of disbelief and a shuffling of feet in the vast room,

"How in the name of Allah can we do that??" shouted several of the gathered.

"Qom and Natanz!" replied their confident Caliph, *"We capture the nuclear weapons they have developed there and then not only would Iran fall but the rest of the Muslim world would join us!"* he continued.

The raising and firing of their AK's signified

their instant agreement with this plan.
The new direction of IC was now clear.

Chapter Eight

As before the offer to join his Caliphate and
march to freedom and victory was put to
those of the deflated Shia's who had the
capacity and strength to fight. The women,
the sick, the elderly and children were spared
the ordeal of further duress or execution as an
encouraging gesture for the men to join IC.
This policy appeared to have the desired
affect as several thousand rallied to their
converted Islamic faith.
What weapons and transport that could be
used was salvaged from the Baghdad mire.

Having poured over the images of the remains
of Baghdad taken by the latest U2 spy-plane
flights, the Pentagon thought not

to exacerbate the situation in Baghdad further and ceased any bombing on built up areas. With the coalition armies proceeding up from Basra in the south and down from Sirnak in the north on the Turkish border, both the Pentagon and United Nations Council agreed to wait until the capital was surrounded and then lay siege to it.

The proposal from General Atocha to issue orders to kill the self proclaimed leader Al-Malouf was soon countermanded by the United Nations Council who, to a man and one woman, displayed their preference to capture Al-Malouf alive and put him on trial in the Hague as a war criminal. The American Joint Chief of Staff could not accept that and fiercely fought for a similar demise to that they had imparted on Osama Bin Laden. In his eyes there could be no hero for future Sunni Muslim followers to rally around and possibly engage in hostage situations in exchange for their leaders release.

After much heated debate it was agreed that no special orders for the safety of Al-Malouf were to be issued and that fate was to be left in charge.

The resolution was passed for a slow circular infiltration of Baghdad, street by street, until only the core of the jihadist army was left and at which point an offer of surrender would be put forward.

Little did the Coalition leadership conceive or even contemplate the possibility of Al-Malouf's proposed strike on Iran to Baghdad's east. This would be a fatal oversight by those who should have known better.

Slowly his forces rallied at various collection points in the eastern suburbs of Baghdad in preparation for the rapid eighty kilometre dash across the Iraqi desert to the small town of Mandali nestling in the foothills of the northern Zagros Mountains on the Iranian border. However before being certain of the American spy-planes announcing to the world of their exodus toward Iran and in a further act of defiance, Al-Malouf ordered an additional wave of his suicide bombers in Syria to immediately return to their European homelands and extend the chaos already engulfing several major cities.

Once again the city of Baghdad was blanketed in darkness as the evening sun descended below the western horizon. Time for the IC force to embark on their 'do or die' mission to take Iran. With the ever defiant Pakistani heading the first convoy aboard his T-72 tank, the four columns of soldiers in their tanks, APC's and Hilux jeeps slipped into the desert night with as much speed as their vehicles would carry them.

The mighty armada of two hundred tanks, ninety APC's, three hundred and twenty Howitzers, mostly scavenged from the remnants of the Iraqi army garrison in Baghdad and hundreds and hundreds of Toyota jeeps, lorries and family cars carried the estimated strength of thirty five thousand jihadists plundered across the cool desert floor toward Mandali.

It was but a brief spell of time before the U2 piloted by Captain Sweller spotted the cloud of dust gathering to the east of Baghdad through his infra-red radar,

"Red 1 to base. Spotted mass movement east towards Iranian border."

Seconds later this information reached the ears of the Pentagon and a few seconds following that to the ears of the Council of United Nations and the Command of NATO who were heavily engaged in the international military build up encroaching towards Baghdad.

"He's breaking out for the safety of the Zagros" Atocha suggested to the President.
"But they are in Iran!" exclaimed O'Shea.

Given the political ramifications of that situation President O'Shea hurriedly arranged for a call to be put through to President Akbari in Tehran. Meanwhile he ordered an immediate resumption of air attacks on the convoy from the Gerald Ford but fully realising that with the time taken for the F-18's or Tomahawk cruise missiles to get to east Baghdad there would be precious little opportunity of strikes without encroaching into Iranian airspace. This was not, as yet, authorised.

Akbari would be given this dubious honour to take-out the IC army upon his own soil. This was consequently agreed by Tehran who ordered the 3rd Tactical Unit based at Shahrokhi Air Base, Hamadan to get airborne and fly west.

Up to this point Israeli Prime Minister Jacob Benayoun and his Cabinet spent weeks sat nervously in the knesset in Jerusalem waiting to see how the Iraq theatre would play out. They had had enough trouble with Hamas in Gaza of late and were not anxious to extend their engagements for a while, unless pressed to do so! However, when Mossad (Israeli Intelligence) received the intelligence that IC was moving into Iran a full Cabinet meeting was convened by Benayoun for that afternoon.

For years the authority in Tehran had vowed to wipe Israel of the map and had used it's denied 'open secret' of the development of nuclear weapons as a PR deterrent. On several occasions Benayoun had drawn up strike plans to fly to Qom and Natanz (the nuclear research factories) and take them out but global public opinion had been too great to antagonise, up till now!

For hours the Israeli Council discussed any advantages they might select from the ongoing invasion of Iran by IC. Was it an invasion? Was it just protection from Coalition strikes? or was it to reform in the Zagros Mountains? All these scenarios were postulated by none unanimously agreed upon and certainly no strike plan at this time had been approved.

Al-Malouf's watch read 0005 hrs as he made the first sighting of the dark house line of Mandali in the early morning desert mist. He radioed the other two columns to bypass the

town and meet up at the Iranian border on
the road to Eslamabad where he would join
them after passing through Mandali to
procure some more recruits willing to convert
to his cause.

The five Iranian Air Force Phantom F4D's
were the first aircraft to arrive overhead the
IC armada just as much of it was crossing the
border. Being only a first generation fighter
with a limited capacity payload and a
performance not conducive to high
manoeuvrability the damage they inflicted on
the vast IC army was limited with the killing
of an estimated one hundred jihadists and the
loss of one tank plus a few jeeps. However, the
same damage limitation could not be said of
the Iranian aircraft as three were brought
down either with captured
RPG's or the barrage of machine gun bullets.
The two remaining F4's depleted of their
payload turned back for Hamadan.
Meanwhile in Mandali Al-Malouf had
successfully managed to recruit several
hundred more to his cause before driving out
of the town to meet up with the balance of his
force at the Iranian border.
The dawn light rose gently to reveal the
extent of the Zagros ahead complete with it's

covering of snow. There was only one pass through the rugged range which was the road to Eslamabad and Hamadan. The IC had no choice than to proceed through this natural feature panning out everything, except the tanks, on either side on the tarmac so as not to present an easy target for the inevitable Iranian Air Force.

The higher they climbed with thicker the snow became too such a point that it was impossible for the pick-up's and APC's to make progress across the valley slopes and were forced down onto the clear road.

Two more squadrons of Phantom F4D's were scrambled as well as four Battalions of troops mobilised from the garrison at Bakharan.

The engagement by the F4's was more successful on this occasion due to the higher concentration of the IC men and machines. Much damage was inflicted on Al-Malouf without the loss of a single Iranian aircraft. But still the IC progress east through the valley continued unabated towards Eslamabad. More air strikes were to follow before the town came into sight later that evening. Al-Malouf ploughed through his first Iranian town with great ease. With no preparation and no military presence any form of resistance would have been futile. All the Pakistani wanted from the mountain town was a stock-up of food and water for his army. Not wishing to drive the population to arms or anger and leaving them at his rear, no lives or hostages were taken. The following day all haste toward Bakhtaran was the order of the day.

In the relative placitude of Jerusalem Prime Minister Benayoun sat patiently with his Chief's of Staff correlating the latest batch of American intelligence sent to them by flash transmission. Realising that IC were heading towards the capital of Iran and in the highly unlikely event that they were to succumb to the Sunni Muslim onslaught Benayoun was becoming very nervous and concerned about their position on the Middle-East stage. Coping with the Iranian threats had been well within their capabilities up to this point but the innate hatred of the Jews by IC would present a completely different situation should the Iranian regime be overturned. It was time for Benayoun to put the Israeli Air Force on full battle alert in anticipation of a change of circumstance.

O'Shea was fully aware of the relatively unabated progress of IC through the Zagros

Mountains and along with the coalition leaders felt powerless to intervene militarily whilst the jihadists were on Iranian soil. The question of the security of Iran's nuclear programme was beginning to be of more than a major concern to the leadership of the west. It was pressure from O' Shea that led to the Council of the United Nations approaching President Akbari for permission for the American Air Force to fly drone missions over the IC positions to enable accurate surveillance. Tehran agreed provided they were unarmed and would be kept informed with up-to-date intel.

The Commander of Creech Air Base in Nevada was ordered to ready two MQ-9 Reaper drones for immediate deployment to the Gerald Ford in the Gulf.

Suffering several further relatively ineffectual Iranian air strikes Al-Malouf continued his relentless progress towards Bakhtaran through the deep crisp, white snow. The average forward speed of his army had slowly dramatically as he neared the summit of the mountain pass in the unforgiving Zagros. The cold was causing much distress amongst many of the followers, especially to the women who had been forced to accompany many of the soldiers as company, including the harim of Al-Malouf. The worst would be over within a day as the city lights caressing the evening sky with a warm reddy hue came into view.

The city looked large. The importance and facilities of this obscure place were unknown to the man from Lahore or any of his fellow Syrian leaders. Not wishing to delay his campaign on Tehran or risk losing too many more men or machines, Al-Malouf decided to skirt around Bakhtaran, leave it in relative peace and proceed at pace to the very important city of Hamadan. Once that had fallen to the Sunni onslaught there would be little to impede the road to Tehran.

The sighting of American Reapers low in the sky threw a sense of panic into the vast army of Al-Malouf's followers. Never had they anticipated the presence of American forces in Iran. Memories of his brother's death from a drone attack on the Afghanistan border re-ignited Al-Malouf's hate of the Americans. Little did he know of the capability of these unmanned machines ..few did. It was not until one of the Reapers had flown several missions over his forces without dropping any form of payload that Al-Malouf realised it's mission was pure surveillance. It was clear that Tehran had not given permission for the Americans to strike on Iranian soil. This was pleasing to IC as all they had to contend with was the rather half-hearted efforts from the Iranians. If the air strikes got no worse than those he had already suffered then the sacking of Tehran would be an easy undertaking. What Al-Malouf was not aware of, was the amassing military defence awaiting him on the outskirts of Hamadan!

Anticipating the next passing of one of the drones Al-Malouf ordered a bank of his men with shoulder APG's to bring it down. It would be an easy target as it's cruising speed was only in the region of three hundred miles per hour when holding a steady course.

The ground pilot of the drone, sat in his comfortable cabin environment in Nevada, was suddenly surprised when his viewing screen went fuzzy before going blank. He sat back in his chair for a second before advising his commander of his drone's demise. Orders would have to be issued for a replacement to be sent out to the carrier in the Gulf. This would all take time. Meanwhile Admiral Jones, perched in his control tower supervising deck top operations in the afternoon warmth of the Persian Gulf, was instructed to double the operational time of his remaining Reaper.

Still the Iranian Air Force used their best endeavours with their ageing Phantom F4's but accomplished little to inhibit the slow but sure progress of Al-Malouf's hoard.

News of this 'Hannibal' encroachment into Iran filtered into the media which further served to increase the flight of 'would be' jihadists into the conflict.

In Baghdad the coalition were recovering from the awful scenes of devastation they encountered and did what they could to improve the situation. Humanitarian help had been arranged to fly into the airport now sufficiently dry to allow the safe landing of cargo aircraft stuffed full of gifted food, medical supplies and temporary accommodation in the form of tents and portable huts.

The violence and disruption in many of Europe's major cities was becoming intolerable as the police were becoming unable to control public street anger even with the use of guns. The point of military troops being ordered to intervene was close.

In France a full division of L'Armee was deployed to a base just fifteen kilometres from Paris in full readiness to march into the city and qwell the rapidly escalating Parisian mayhem.

For some strange reason an undercurrent of anti-Semitism began to rear it's ugly head in several cities throwing a state of nervousness into the minds of so many European immigrant Jews. Hundreds had even taken the decision to return to Israel for personal safety putting increasing pressure upon Benayoun to start showing his colours in the growing middle-east conflict. The progress of IC within Iran was the sole topic of debate in the Cabinet. One covert decision had been unanimously agreed on which was that Mossad (Secret Service) should immediately dispatch a small secretive force into Iran to monitor the situation and establish the true and exact situation of all Al-Malouf's forces. Later that night a single C-130 Hercules departed Ramat David Air Base heading at altitude across Jordanian and Iraqi airspace. Once established on the Iranian border around Mandali the dozen or so Mossad agents and their equipment would be jettisoned from the rear cargo door. They would free-fall for as long as possible into Iranian territory landing as far as possible along the trail that IC had recently taken.

Reports began to trickle into Jerusalem of

suicide bombing activity in the northern Egyptian town of Al-Arish. Being very close to the Sinai border this was beginning to be of extreme concern to the Israeli military as it meant a possible remote IC build up to their south. If this bombing proved to be a sustained activity with a threat directed northwards and not just an isolated incident on the Egyptian coast it would require devoting much military resources to the south as well as the north of Israel.

Chapter Nine

The battle of Hamadan opened with a salvo of 125mm and 155mm shell bursts from the Iranian Zulfiger MBT-1 and T-72 tanks which landed amidst the oncoming IC T-72's. The Iranian army had taken up a defensive position on the foothills of the Alvand Mountains which stood between the very ancient city of Hamadan and the invading jihadists. Two lines comprising of a mixture of fifty Zulfiger and forty T-72 tanks flanked by a division of M-109 tracked 155mm Howitzers had anxiously awaited the arrival of Al-Malouf and his army of thugs. Joining in the mighty battle from the sky were several more Phantom F4's which screamed in low across the mountain to unleash another round of five hundred pounders on the invaders.

The initial pounding from the barrage of one hundred and thirty Iranian barrels filled the approaching multi-national force with awe and panic. None of the IC force had anticipated such an impressive show of force from the impoverished Iran. Many of the IC tanks and pick-ups were destroyed beyond further use adding to the balls of flame and columns of smoke as they exploded.

Caught somewhat on open ground and feeling cold and tired from the perilous journey from Baghdad Al-Malouf hurriedly issued orders for his remaining tanks , Howitzers and pick-ups to scatter and to remain out of range of the Iranian armaments forcing the Iranians to move forward into open ground. His RPG (rocket propelled grenade) team was further ordered to concentrate their efforts purely on downing the Iranian aircraft. The battle scene rapidly became one of chaos and a hell hole on earth. Both sides exchanging fire from hundreds of tanks and howitzers anxiously attempting to outmanoeuvre it's adversary and score a kill.

The Midday sun was blocked out by the perpetual black smoke and the smell of cordite pervading the air for miles around. The eyes of the footsoldiers on both sides and those aboard the IC Toyotas began to weep with the toxicity of the environmental air. Two Phantoms screamed out of the sun in close formation with full cannons ablaze tearing up the ground and anything in the spray path before them. The scattering Toyotas stood no chance and were annihilated in the process. Bodies flew across the snow covered floor. Round after round left the barrels of the professional Iranian tanks and howitzers tearing the scattering invaders to pieces. The IC army appeared to be on the point of collapse until the Iranian machinery began to move forward from their entrenched position in the Alvand foothills which opened up a weakness in their defence. Al-Malouf quickly saw this and ordered his fast moving Toyota force to drive around and behind the oncoming armour and attack it from the rear.

With the thick of the battle now at its height and confusion reining throughout the mayhem, now was the time for part two of Al-Malouf's plan to be activated.

Inviting his most trusted leadership of two Pakistani and one Syrian commanders to join him aboard his T-72 sheltering in the lea of a nearby rock the Caliph instructed them to gather up their remaining Toyota pick up force and follow his Russian tank east away from the main fight.

Using the copious quantity of black smoke as a covering screen the small convoy of one T-72 trailed by a line of twenty four jeeps each containing three or four soldiers, slipped away from the frey towards the lowlands of the eastern Alvand .. destination Qom and Natanz about one hundred miles away.

Observing the plumes of black smoke rising to the heavens in the distance whilst pedalling their specially designed lightweight mini bikes along the icy mountain road the Mossad agents realised that the Islamic jihadists had encountered Iranian resistance. Their pace increased to an almost inhuman level in order to directly observe the fighting before an outcome had been achieved. It was important to report back to Jerusalem the exact situation.

Armed with the knowledge that the two sides were in actual conflict gave the Israeli Cabinet a distorted sense of ease. All the councillors inner thoughts were that each side might destroy the other entirely thus relinquishing the threat upon themselves.

To complicate matters even further the radical Muslim group in Gaza, Hamas, had been informed of the IC incursion into Iran and were fully aware of the uprising in Sinai to the south of Israel so decided this to be a good opportunity to take some potshots at Israel from the west.

When the short range rockets began to fall on the Israeli cultural capital Benayoun flew into a rage and called his complete military machine to RED1 alert. All reservists were to be called up, all leave cancelled and the release of all weapons sanctioned. Israel was ordered onto a full war footing.

Progress had been good for Al-Malouf as his escape from the battlefield under the cover of smoke appeared to have been successful. Now twenty kilometres from the ensuing carnage a peaceful environment enveloped his select group. The going up to that point had been twisty and rugged but as the mountain gave up it's control to the undulating plateau dusk began to fall. The cover of darkness would once again come to the assistance of Al-Malouf as he carefully traversed the relatively level dusty ground. Any dust trails kicked up by the T-72's tracks or Toyota wheels would be lost in the murkiness. He felt confident on a covert approach to his ultimate targets in Qom and Natanz.

As dawn began to break through the early morning mist and with only few kilometres to the research facility at Qom Al-Malouf called for a halt to make camp. Before embarking on his assault of the nuclear factories he wanted his group to rest, eat and plan a strategy of attack. A group of trees served as cover from any marauding aircraft.

With no intelligence as to how his army was fairing against the Iranians back at Hamadan Al-Malouf continued planning his approach to both the factories, Natanz being just a few kilometres to the south-east of Qom.

An hour was required for the laptop to lock onto a wi-fi signal, much to the surprise of the IC team who had expected the Iranian authorities to have cut off the internet system in the event of hostilities on their territory. The google search of the two nuclear facilities threw up detailed images of the factories and their surrounding environment.

After due deliberation with his colleagues and it was finally agreed that the force would split into two with Al-Malouf in the T-72 tank leading the assault on the more arduous target of Qom whilst Hassan and ten Toyotas would carry on to the 'soft' factory at Natanz. A coordinated time of attack was further agreed for 2000 hrs that night at which time both factories would be approached under the cover of darkness. Following several hours rest the two units then bid each other good luck and proceeded to their assigned targets.

The view of the battlefield from the secluded ridge gave little away as to who had the upper hand. Peering intently through his 10x60 camouflage infra red binoculars Major Steinback could clearly observe many, many burnt our tanks still smouldering on the plateau beneath but as to their livery he could not be sure. Bodies were littered throughout the area. Fighting was still in progress.

As to what action, if any, he should take Steinback decided to make camp at his present position and inform Jerusalem of what he could see. The absence of the IC leader from the field of action had not been noted by the Mossad commander as his arrival at the ridge was far too late.

In the weak Mediterranean sun more action was underway as Hamas were throwing short range Iranian built Faj-5r rockets at the rate of one a minute as well as several of their newly acquired Syrian Khaibar-1 long range missiles into the built up area of Jerusalem and Tel Aviv. Benayoun had no choice than to respond with a heavy hand and so embarked on all out offensive on Gaza. Both air strikes and a tank advance were ordered. This action only prompted a further escalation of violence in the Sinai with Egyptian troops and tanks now advancing towards the Jewish State. An Arab v Jew war was once again in full operation.

1930 hrs: Al-Malouf had, much to his surprise, journeyed safely without detection over the Zagros foothills and was poised in the darkness ready to advance on his target of Fordo, thirty miles south of Qom. Using the Iranians own wi-fi signal from the research facility he once again engaged the internet to establish a more detailed layout of the factory and from that decided that and attack directly through the rather solitary and unprotected main gate would be the best strategy. Unbeknown to Al-Malouf, Hassan had adopted the same plan of attack albeit on a much more compact target.

The overall layout of the Qom nuclear plant was not what had been expected. Almost nothing showed above the ground. Virtually no buildings, except for a few around the main gate. Surrounded by a series of three high parallel barbed wire fences the site from the eye of a passing spy satellite would have been difficult to interpolate. This was supposed to have been a secret establishment for the enrichment of Uranium for so called 'civilian' purposes!

As the second hand clicked passed twelve Al-Malouf made his move by breaking cover driving his T-72, followed by the balance of his convoy, onto the approach road and applied full power to the huge 750hp V12 engine. The first shot made direct contact with the reception block housed to the side of the main gate. It exploded into a million pieces sending debris high into the sky in a ball of flame. The underground factory sirens sounded alerting what security guards were on the surface of the premises. They would prove highly inadequate against the barrage of bullets from the compilation of the T-72's machine gun and the Toyota's KPV 14.5 mm guns. The huge strong steel gates presented no obstacle to the twenty five tons of Russian tank as it smashed through it like a hot knife through butter. Guards armed with their KL-7's and MPT-9 assault guns appeared from every surface doorway but were simply no match for the fire-power of the Toyota mounted KPV's which tore the Iranian foot soldiers to shreds. Another shot from the T-72 saw the utter destruction of one of the very few surface buildings. Within just a few seconds the surface of the facility was clearly under IC control. The next step was the assault on the massive underground section. Access through their selected entrance proved very easy for the ruthless IC team as a short burst from one of the KPV machine guns simply annihilated the entrance door. Led by Al-Malouf himself the group of two hundred heavily armed jihadists poured down the concrete steps and into the modern and complicated intestines of the nuclear research institute. Every attempt by both armed and unarmed staff to protect the valuable holdings was met with a hail of lead from the militants AK-47s. Blood spattered the walls and ran down the shiny corridors as one after another of the technicians felt the wrath of the Syrian's anger. With no knowledge of Farsi, the language of Iran, none of the directional signs or door notations were understandable to Al-Malouf or any of his followers. Together with their limited knowledge of nuclear technicalities the jihadists began to loose focus of their objective ..what were they to steal?

A certain silence began to fall as more and more of the Iranian technicians threw up their hands in surrender. Not having the same bloodthirsty ideology as the invaders the men in white coats saw no reason to die unnecessarily. Calm now reined with the residue of the factory staff safely locked in one of the offices. IC were now in full control of the vast underground plant.

Once a Reece of the heart of the operations amongst the hundreds of centrifuges had been complete Al-Malouf was no wiser as to what might be construed as a 'dirty bomb'. The complexity and bewilderment of the abundance of signage, apart from the international radiation symbol plastered everywhere, was totally alien to him and his group. With no other option open he arranged for the incarcerated staff to be roughly interrogated in pursuit of one or two of them being able to converse in a language the terrorists could understand.

It was an elderly, grey haired guy wearing a bloodstained white coat that eventually broke into English which Al-Malouf understood very well. Separated from his colleagues in another room and with a pistol held hard against the rear of his head he offered to be cooperative.

Al-Malouf then demanded the location of the bombs that had been developed. The terrified scientist answered,

"There are no bombs, no bombs. This is an civilian project for nuclear electricity!"

This Al-Malouf did not believe and ordered his man to cock his pistol in readiness to fire a bullet into the Iranian's head. With genuine distress and panic in his voice the elderly man repeated,

"No bombs sir no bombs this is an electric generating plant only. The mention of bomb making was a bluff against the Israeli. It was a bluff...a bluff!! I tell the truth."

"Put a bullet in the man's leg" Al-Malouf

ordered in Syrian.

Bang and the scientist reeled to the floor in excruciating pain.

"I will ask again . Where is the bomb?"

Al-Malouf demanded feeling sure that the prisoner would now speak the truth.

"No bomb. I tell you the truth I tell you the truth!"

The truth was now out Iran never did develop a nuclear bomb or warhead. It was just one huge international bluff! to frighten Israel. What was Al-Malouf to do now?

As dawn came up Major Steinback was presented with the aftermath of the battle of Hamadan. Thousands lay dead amongst the smouldering vehicles. The scene of carnage lay still enticing the Mossad group to break cover from the ridge and walk through the mess.

So many heads had been parted from their torsos. The awful smell and onset of nauseousness hit all the hardened Israeli soldiers but it was the straight line of fifty headless bodies lying unceremoniously on the ground that sank them to their knees. Never before had they seen such barbarity. It was clear to Steinback that IC had won the day.

On a more focussed investigation Steinback found evidence that what remained of the IC army had continued on east. In his professional estimation there could only be one destination that they were heading for...

...Tehran.

He had to advise his Prime Minister of this development.

On receiving this not unpredicted intel whilst still accessing the implications of the onslaught from Hamas in Gaza and the procession of the Egyptian Brotherhood up from the Sinai, Benayoun and his Cabinet hit upon the idea of taking advantage of the turmoil and obvious panic in Iran and take out the main nuclear plant at Qom. This agenda gradually took hold until the complete Cabinet were in full agreement to order Major Steinback to proceed with his team onto Qom and destroy it.

After some joint map referencing in the soft morning light the Israeli team, glad to be leaving the scene of horror, mounted their mini bikes and pedalled furiously in an eastward direction.

Fraught with frustration over the absence of any nuclear or any fissionable material that he could use or modify to blackmail Tehran and the coalition into submission, the IC leader took succour from a thought that suddenly flashed through his mind.... if Tehran could hold Israel to heel for so many years with a bluff .... why could not he?

Embedded with a new lease of interest Al-Malouf hurriedly arranged the construction of an oblong device, about the size of an average man, to be covered in several radiation decals. With the object complete, having taken an hour or so to construct out of a oxygen cylinder found in a cupboard in the centrifuge hall with three spherical balls welded to it, Al-Malouf had it mounted on a table in the hall.

The short video he was now about to shoot with the aid of one of his colleagues and his smartphone would have to be convincing so one of the prisoners wearing a white coat was forcibly brought to the centrifuge hall. Ordered to stand alongside the table the scientist awaited the entrance of the IC leader. In walked Al-Malouf bearing his full black outfit and bandana whilst carrying one of his IC flags. The filming started. Al-Malouf spoke towards the tiny microphone of the smartphone in English,

" *You will see that I speak to you from the*

nuclear plant in Qom here in Iran and this is one of the nuclear WMD's (weapons of mass destruction) that I now have in my control. I have ordained that my Caliphate include Tehran and I intend to be there within days to claim my throne. If there is any resistance then I will detonate at least one of these weapons in a major Iranian city. Also the coalition will stop all air strikes upon my IC forces from this point or again I will explode one of my weapons. To prove I am serious this man will now pay the price" and with a swift movement of his right hand withdrew a knife from under his dishdasha and plunged it deep into the scientist's throat.

"Post that to youtube!" he then ordered of the smartphone operator.

Not wishing to waste anymore time in the confines of the research facility where he felt he could be targeted by an American cruise missile Al-Malouf dictated that all the prisoners be executed so as not to be able to tell the world that his device was a fake,! before bidding a hasty retreat back up to the outside world.

The relatively short journey of sixty kilometres north to Tehran would require his force to skirt around the mountainous glens of Hasan Aqa and Furdu Peaks into which the research plant had been covertly constructed before being able to speed across the Central Desert to the Iranian capital.

Upon being informed of the contents of the youtube video which had immediately been picked up by the NSA (National Security Authority) in the States and GCHQ in United Kingdom President O'Shea went puce with anger. The position in which he now found himself was both difficult and embarrassing, to say the least. Faced with a threat of at least one dirty nuclear device in the hands of blood thirsty terrorists was every national leader's nightmare.
With his hands tied like this what would he be expected to do?
The same embarrassment also faced the leaders of the coalition forces.
In view of the incalculable repercussions should Al-Malouf's threat be carried out, all coalition hostilities in the middle-east were brought to a temporary rest whilst the Councils of The United Nations and NATO hastily convened a joint meeting in New York.
The leader who was most perplexed by the contents of the IC video was Prime Minister Benayoun in Jerusalem. He had just sanctioned the destruction of the research

facility which would now be to no avail as the terrorist Al-Malouf had beaten his Mossad force to it! However, following diligent consideration with his staff he ordered that Steinback be advised via the Satellite phone to still close in on the facility at Qom and fully ensure that all the centrifuges were completely destroyed and any WMD's lying around be destroyed as well.

Chapter Ten

The greatest cause for concern was being heralded in the luxury of the Green House in central Tehran where President Akbari had hurriedly accumulated his Council for a crisis meeting. They faced a situation of terrifying proportions. Advancing from their west was the balance of the IC army with an unknown quantity of tanks and from the south a force of unknown strength with two fake WMD's.

The conundrum that faced Akbari was that if he capitulated to the threat of a nuclear device, which the Israelis were led to believe to have been developed, he would have let the terrorists into his city without a fight, but if he attempted to stop the advancing IC army and Al-Malouf never detonated a device, the world would then know of their (Iran's) nuclear bluff. Following that revelation Israel could never again be subjugated by Iran. The minutes ticked by as the Council prevaricated over what best action to take. Councillor Derafsh put forward the idea of asking the Americans for help. Akbari immediately suppressed that suggestion. With memories of the hostage crisis of 1981 still set deep in the Iranian mindset the requesting of American help would not be accepted by the general public. However, the possibility of seeking help from certain members of the coalition might well skirt public objections should the situation get out of control.

The first firm decision made was to double check that the internet across the whole country was off-air. All were agreed that the population should know as little as possible about what was about to hit them. Panic in the streets was the last situation any of them wanted. The next decision was to consult the Ayatollah and rapidly mobilise the elite Revolutionary Guard (IRGC), who by chance were based at Bidganeh some thirty kilometres west of Tehran and meet the threat of the oncoming IC whose three factions, unbeknown to President Akbari, had already reunited on the desert plains near the village of Aveh some ten kilometres south of Saveh.

For the last immediate decision the use of two of their latest prototype Fotros drones was authorised to fly over the region west of Tehran and reconnoitre for the exact whereabouts of the enemy's positions.

The council had confidence in the ability of their elite IRGC guards, having the men and might, to stop and eliminate the balance of the IC threat once the terrorist's position and strength had been established and a suitable battleground located. It sat at the back of Akbari's mind that a final confrontation would eventually have to take place as he could not see the Pakistani leader of IC backing away from his bluff.

Within the hour the full Council including the Ayatollah had succumbed to the same conclusion. The final battle for the future of

Iran was to be fought within a matter of hours!

Al-Malouf, having reformatted with his triumphant, but severely depleted force from Hamadan and his colleagues from Natanz who, like their leader, found no evidence of any nuclear weapons, had now to plan the final advance of his campaign to capture Tehran. Not sure whether his internet bluff would work or not played heavily upon his mind. He too fully realised the plight he had placed upon the Iranian leadership. Would they be willing to admit to the world the bluff of their protestations or suppress this news and fight for their survival.

The desert night was once again drawing in as the IC prepared to bed down for the night to awaken fresh in the morning for the push into Tehran itself.

It was then that one of the strange drones swooped low over the encamped IC force at three hundred feet catching the jihadists off guard. It's slow speed , subdued noise level and low altitude allowed no warning of it's approach.

"Shit (or some such word in Urdu) *I had no idea the Iranians had drones. Now they know our exact position and situation"*

spelled out Al-Malouf to his senior staff. We start off at very first light.

With the drone intel laid before him President Akbari ordered the IRGC to head for and dig in at the base of the small hilltop of Eslam Shahr-e Tanbur and intercept the Syrian jihadists. He was convinced that they would have to pass by this rift rising from the desert floor for an incursion into the south western suburbs of Tehran. He further ordered the Air Force Squadrons from Hamadan, Esfahan and Mehr-abad International Airport be ready to strike at first light. Little sleep was had by those in command that night.

Five thousand miles away in Washington DC President O'Shea arose from his somewhat disturbed slumber in the Presidential suite of the White House having been advised of
Al-Malouf's video broadcast the previous evening. The feeling of helplessness was overwhelming not only to him but also to his whole senior military staff. The thought of a bloodthirsty terrorist having a couple of 'dirty bombs' in his possession was pressurising to say the least. To then have that terrorist within Iranian territory, of all

places, completely tied his hands. The British Prime Minister plus the other leaders within the coalition all felt the same utter frustration! A waiting game ensued.

Very tired and hungry from the prolonged bike journey across the snow covered mountain road the Mossad force finally approached the research facility at Fordow near Qom. Surprised by the solitude of the area Steinback approached with extreme caution.

Crawling on their hands and knees under the cover of darkness they finally managed to observe the destruction of the main gated entrance. Once inside the darkened base and faced with the multitudes of bodies strew across the concrete it was obvious to the Mossad Commander that the facility was deserted. He ordered his men to follow him into the underground section where they found the Iranian staff lying in pools of blood in the centrifuge hall. Rightly or wrongly Steinback ordered that the scene of the mass execution be included in the extensive filming of the interior of the hall. He wanted to secure damning evidence for any international war crimes tribunal that might be convened in the future concerning the trial of any IC leaders. In the meanwhile an intensive search was made for any evidence of weapons grade material. None was found. Steinback had then only two conclusions to report back to Jerusalem. Either Al-Malouf had removed the entire stock of WMD's, which he concluded highly unlikely or the Iranians never had any and the pretence they had was a massive international bluff. Once the film had been completed and all the explosive charges strategically placed Steinback contacted Benayoun on the sat-phone and informed him of the situation and awaited final orders to blow the plant sky high. As fortune would have it Benayoun was fast asleep so the Deputy Prime Minister took the call and confirmed that the plant not, repeat NOT be destroyed in light of the new revelations. Steinback was ordered to evacuate the plant to a save distance and remain undetected until further orders. He was however to stay within range of the detonation remote control for the next twelve hours should the requirement of complete destruction of the facility be forthcoming. The quick thinking Deputy PM knew the Iranian authorities would shortly be on the scene and if the centre was still intact the presence of other intruders would not be suspected and Mossad's activity could continue in secret.

Within the hour Benayoun was awakened and duly informed of the latest position. Hurriedly he countermanded his deputy's order. Having been an ex-Mossad operative himself he realised that the Iranians would eventually locate and recognise the explosives planted in the factory which would immediately alert them to the recent presence of an Israeli force. The new order to blow the factory was then relayed to Steinback.

As the charges received Steinback's remote signal, detonation occurred and up went the underground complex in a huge fireball reaching hundreds of feet into the dark sky. The combination of the C4 explosive and various chemicals involved in the centrifuge enrichment hall created such a shock wave that the ground above simply collapsed into a vast crater. It was Benayoun's hope that the destruction occurred before the Iranians had arrived and had located the explosives.

The completion of Steinback's sat-phone message ordered him to proceed towards Tehran and covertly report on any situation he might find.

Dawn rose at 0530hrs on the cold plains around Tehran and was privy to the preparations of Al-Malouf and his IC army for their march onto Tehran. In his wisdom the canny Pakistani greengrocer anticipated that there had to be an Iranian army lying in wait for him somewhere between his present position and Tehran. To this end he lay awake all night contriving a plan. Requesting the presence of his senior colleagues to his tent Al-Malouf outlined his strategy.

The tanks and Howitzers were to make a direct north-easterly approach across the desert with ten thousand men following close behind kicking up as much dust as possible using blankets, tree branches or just their feet. Al-Malouf wanted to fool the Iranian army into thinking that all the IC were in one place and in a greater strength than they might have calculated. The huge dust cloud would also have the added benefit of hindering the cameras on any drones that would inevitably appear and diffuse the targets for any Phantom F4 pilots that attempted to lock on any air to ground missiles.

As the armada of T-72's, APC's and Howitzers followed by an army of soldiers set off amidst a tsunami of dust into the morning light Al-Malouf with his multitude of fast moving Toyota pick-up's, lorries and cars held back giving the slower moving tanks a chance to cover some distance. As the enormous dust cloud slowly drifted below the horizon the roar of hundreds of diesel engines starting up filled the air in what was left of the IC overnight camp. Directing half of the mechanised force to proceed in a direction to the left of the cloud Al-Malouf himself lead the other half to the right. His intention to remain as covert as possible letting the tank force take the Iranian pounding whilst his Japanese pick-ups slipped around either side of the inevitable battlefield. By keeping their speed below forty miles per hour any dust thrown up from the hard desert floor would be minimal.

It only took around two hours from their departing the camp-site before the first wave of F-4's came screaming out of the morning sun at breakneck speed. The payloads of five hundred pounders they delivered presented a truly terrifying sight taking out many tanks and howitzers along with a few hundred foot soldiers in the process. Several aircraft got caught in the wall of lead sent high in the sky by the IC tank machine gunners but still the armada drove on. Then a second wave of twenty aircraft, anxious to deliver their barrels of sunshine, flew low over the dust cloud. By now the IC gun crews had measure of the attacking aircraft's height and successfully downed seven F-4's on that attack alone.

No sooner than the third wave of aircraft appeared in the morning sky the lead IC tank drivers could clearly make out the Iranian tank force laying in wait in the shade of a hillock some three kilometres directly ahead.

The relatively inexperienced IRGC commander had had the oncoming wall of sand dust visible in his binoculars for some twenty minutes, however, having learnt of the mistaken decision for the Iranian tanks to move forward and engage the IC force at Hamadan so very recently, remained steadfast resisting the temptation to move forward. The protection of his rear by the Eslam Shahr-e hillock he considered too valuable to loose.

On realising the Iranian commanders tactic the lead IC T-72 tank commander, Al-Diri, slowed his force down in the forlorn hope of enticing the Iranians out to play from their intractable position. The consequence of this reduction in their advance now gave the

Iranian Air Force more time for another two waves of attack both with bombs and on these occasions with ten second bursts of their 20mm Vulcan cannon which ripped the IC soldiers on the ground to ribbons amidst the chocking dust.

Appreciating that his force was rapidly becoming vulnerable Al-Diri had no other tactical choice than to proceed and engage the Iranian tank force head on.

Far across to the left and right of the battlefield Al-Malouf's Japanese jeep armies were covertly circling around Eslam Shahr-e and heading towards Tehran, the tall buildings of which had just become visible on the horizon in the eyepiece of Al-Malouf's binoculars.

The ensuing exchange of fire between the multitude of tanks and howitzers under the shadow of Eslam Shahr-e became very intense with inevitable losses being sustained by both sides. But still the Iranian commander held firm his position in the lee of the hillock. For what must have seemed like an eternity to those encased in their armoured steel machines, but in reality was more like half an hour, the horror of tank warfare continued.

With not having too much to offer at this

stage of the battle the IC footsoldiers held back out of range of the Iranian Zulfigar and T-72's waiting for the equivalent Iranian guards to show their face on the field of battle.

Still shells rained down tearing the desert floor apart as the Syrian armour grew ever closer to the Iranian position. Having no soldiers in their near vicinity creating the protective dust screen the IC tanks became an easier target for the more experienced Iranian sharp shooters. The battle was beginning to turn in the Iranian favour. Still the IC advanced into the jaws of the immovable IRGC. It was very tempting for Al-Diri to withdraw from the frey and attempt to proceed onto Tehran but the thought of the Iranian tanks coming after him in pursuit was more terrifying than facing them head on.

Sat in what he thought was the relative safety of his mighty Russian T-72 tank Al-Diri somehow knew of the 125mm shell that was earmarked for him! When it hit the forward section of his turret the force of the explosion lifted it clean away from main body of the T-72 and deposited it on the desert floor. Nothing would ever be found of the Syrian tank group commander.

Soon both sides were so enveloped in such close contact that it was impossible for either to shoot for fear of hitting their own..now it was time for the thousands of the foot brigade to engage in close mortal combat.

As the residue of the IC jihadists, brandishing their AK's and scimitars,swarmed forward into the fight their nostrils began filling with the stench of spent cordite. Within minutes some twenty thousand religious combatants fought with each other for their cause at close quarters. Both sides carried the dedication and 'want' to win. No compassion was shown. Gradually the ground turned red with the blood of hundreds of dead but as the day wore on it was the sheer determination of the jihadists, having lost their commander, that delivered them the upper hand. The white flag of surrender was raised above the IRGC's commander's Zulfigar. The cost of victory was heavy, very heavy indeed leaving only twenty two tanks, one hundred and four howitzers and twenty APC's on the final Syrian tally-up. The cost in men was equally devastating to the IC having lost maybe, five to five and a half thousand men.

Without any objection being raised from the joyous army the Pakistani friend of Al-Malouf, Tariq Gajari, immediately assumed command of the victorious IC group. His first order before proceeding onto Tehran was to execute all the defeated Iranian officers. Not supporting quite such a ruthless streak as his friend, Gajari allowed the few surviving Iranian NCO's and soldiers their freedom but not before removing their boots and trousers! With no weapons, no boots and no trousers what danger could they now present, so Gajari thought. The handful of usable captured tanks were quickly absorbed into his inventory.

By this time one of Al-Malouf's column of Toyota jeeps had been spotted, firstly by a passing drone followed by a couple of F-4's holding a few kilometres off the tank battleground at Eslam Shahr-e. With the proximity of the jeeps being so close to Tehran both F-4's immediately engaged with bursts from their 20mm Vulcan cannon. Several Toyotas and their occupants were taken out before the pilots had to return to Hamadan Air Base to re-arm. In the meanwhile the lead pilot informed his base of the closeness of so many jeeps to the outskirts of Tehran.

Once President Akbari received news of this sighting a sense of panic set in as he realised that almost nothing would now stand in the way of an invasion of his beloved capital city. His normally dependable Revolutionary Guards had failed in their bid to eliminate the IC.

With great reluctance , having solicited full agreement from the Council, he had no other option than to sound the city's emergency sirens and activate all National Guards and Police within the city. Accessing that Al-Malouf would strike from the south-west all armed forces were ordered to the suburbs of Mehr Abad, Shad Abad and Esmail Abad where they were to engage the invading jihadists with as much vigour as they could muster. Other Air Bases throughout Iran were ordered to relent their present duties and provide whatever air support they could.

Chapter Eleven

With what remained of his ground force sat safely aboard all the serviceable mechanised armour Gajari advanced his force west around the rocky hillock to turn north east at the earliest opportunity and meet up with his leader on the outskirts of Tehran. Breaking radio silence he reported in to Al-Malouf his exact situation and requirement for more fuel but also to further advise him of the death of Al-Diri.

Al-Malouf was saddened with that revelation but was then lifted with the news that his good friend had replaced him. For a second or two memories of his best friend Homayoon Darshinika flashed through his head increasing his resolve to sack Tehran. At that point another, but much larger wave of aircraft swooped from the sky. In lines of four in formation the F-4's strafed the ground with as much lead as they could release. The third line however, Al-Malouf observed, was made up of a different aircraft. Not F-4's but Russian built SU-24's that Iran had stolen from the Iraqi's in the last gulf war. Their 23mm cannon delivered a somewhat harder pack than those from the American Vulcan. The kill rate was not good for the IC. Together with the faster speed of the SU's which made it much more difficult to shot them down with the Toyota mounted machine guns, Al-Malouf had a decision to make.

He ordered his jeeps to spread out and expedite their speed toward the city to take refuge from the aircraft in the shelter of the streets.

Meanwhile whilst under full speed himself he radioed Gajari and told him to use full throttle and make for the south west of Tehran with utmost haste where several public fuel stations would be secured for the refuelling of his tanks.

The sight from the upper bedroom window of number seventy five, being the end house in Beheshi just off the Tehran-Saveh highway right on the edge of the city limits, was terrifying for the young Mina as she stared toward the desert. Hundreds of vehicles flying the black Caliphate flag thundering towards her across the hard desert floor creating a large dust cloud in the process whilst fast jets swooped from the sky unleashing round after round of lead and dropping the occasional bomb.

"Mummy, mummy come and see. What is going on? Mummy I am scarred!" she screamed out in fright. The woman of the house climbed the staircase and entered the bedroom to attend to her daughter's anxiety.

On seeing the same sight as Mina and not being fully appreciative of exactly what was happening she hurriedly grabbed her by the hand and pulled her back down the stairs and out into the street where they both tagged onto the end of the fleeing crowd heading towards the city centre.

The impact from the initial volley of 12.7 mm DshK lead struck Mina's house in the facing west wall obliterating much of the brickwork and window frames. Several of the bullets penetrated the structure and pierced the Butano gas bottles secured in the kitchen. The first pressurised container ignited in an almighty explosion turning the head of the running young Mina back toward her home who saw the huge ball of flame rise skyward tearing sections of the roof clean from the carcase of the main structure. The rush to Azadi Square suddenly increased as panic set in amongst the residents of Beheshi. Shouts and screams in the streets of Tehran, not heard since the the Iran/Iraq war, absorbed the sound of the gunfire emanating from the desert.

Another round of shells hit buildings close to the terrified mother and daughter. A section brickwork splintered through the air catching Mina in her right leg sending her to the ground. As any caring mother would do she turned back and scooped her wounded and badly bleeding daughter from the tarmac then ran as best she could to catch the rest of the crowd.

One after the other the Toyotas entered the relative safety of an urban environment sure in the fact that the Iranian Air Force would not bomb their own capital city even to inhibit the progress of a foreign aggressor. Soon a period of relative tranquillity enveloped the outer suburbs of south west Tehran as Al-Malouf ceased his advance to consolidate his losses and await the arrival of his tank force.

Gajari, with most of his tanks now running on virtual fumes for fuel whilst criss crossing the desert to frustrate the F-4 pilots with their continual air attacks, took solace from the sight of Tehran in their binocular eyepieces. Only a few kilometres to survive thought Gajari.

The sheer tension and heightened emotions of the inexperienced and very frightened tank commander imposed upon him by the continual onslaught from the air whilst in the tight confines of his metal prison led Gajari to order several 125 mm rounds to be randomly placed in the centre of Tehran. The damage that fifty or so tanks and howitzers could cause to a major civilised city needed to be experienced to be able to understood. Building after building was reduced to rubble that morning.

There could be no doubt that each of the eight million population of Tehran were aware that their beautiful city was under attack from an invading force.

For the third time in as many days Steinback came across the handiwork of the terrorist jihadists, at Eslam Shahr-e. The sight of yet another massacre, even of his sworn hated Iranian enemy, sent convulsions of revulsion through his entire body. From the planning and severity of the engagement that had taken place under the cliffs of the desert hillock it had confirmed beyond any doubt to the Israeli Mossad commander that the IC had captured no weapons of mass destruction (WMD). It was abundantly clear that the Iranian claim of being able to 'nuke' Israel at will ...was a bluff. This Steinback reported back to Benayoun in Jerusalem.

The news of the definite bluff was greeted well within the inner circle of the Israeli Government who ordered Steinback to withdraw from Iranian territory back into Iraq where arrangements for an American helicopter pick up would be made. With the threat from Iran somewhat watered down further concentration on matters closer to home in Gaza and Egypt would be more intense. Benayoun also considered it imperative that he shared this information confidentially with President O'Shea in Washington.

Finally having run the gauntlet of many air strikes Gajari and his residual collection of tanks, APC's and howitzers sought refuge in the outer streets of Tehran. Joined by the somewhat distressed Al-Malouf, having lost so much of his original army, plans were implemented to advance to the centre of the city, once the refuelling of the tanks had been completed.
The Police and National Guard in their

attempt to stem the invaders progress had an impossible difficulty in accumulating their forces in the entrance to the districts of Shad Abad, Esmail Abad and Hehr Abad through the fleeing population. Several units did attempt to use the A-Saidi Highway but the traffic proved to dense. The panic in the streets was all to obvious.

The presence of the local dissident hero Yadullah Pisinah to appear in the Green Room had been ordered by the nervous, the very nervous Akbari who was waiting to enlist his co-operation.

Having been greeted like a visiting dignatory upon his arrival at the Sa'dabad Palace before being directed to the adjacent Green Room, Pisinah relished in this opportunity to occupy the seat of decisive power which he assumed was about to be offered to him.

" Salam Yadullah. Come have a seat we have a proposition for you in this very troubled time" spoke Akbari in his ' hour of need' tone. Following a few minutes of private stressed salutations Akbari came forward with his proposition,

"Can you persuade your radical followers and my terrified public to rally around you to fight Al-Malouf? Many will die in the process but the strength of such numbers

can surely defeat the invaders?." Pisinah pondered for a while.

"What do I get out of it if we succeed?" responded Pisinah.

"You will become my Deputy President."

"Make it the Presidency and you have a deal!" retorted the smiling dissident knowing he had Akbari well and truly over a barrel.

The bewildered Akbari did not expect the price to be so high,

"And what of me in your new Iran?"

"You! Prison" commented Pisinah, *"I want you and your Council in prison!"*

The sound of gunfire from the IC tanks and their resulting detonations within the city limits could clearly be heard and seen on the other side of Tehran as Akbari gazed from the window in confused speculation. The idea of languishing in prison did not meet with his delight but if Al-Malouf took the city then his humiliating execution would be guaranteed!

Al-Malouf's tanks, now satisfactorily filled with diesel fuel from the several fuel stations, began to move forward closely followed by the Toyota gun jeeps and foot troops. At first they progressed in just four streets but gradually opened up the front into many more as they closed toward the Azadi Tower in the centre of the city.

On average, every ten or so seconds, each tank released a shell bringing down many buildings in a cloud of smoke and debris. The Toyota based Dshk and KPV machine guns opened up on every sighting of running people tearing their bodies apart as the bullets made contact.

After a few hundred yards of travel through built up areas and crossing the open spaces around Kooy-e Mehrzad and Vali-e Asr the advancing force came to the main railway line running west to east where a token defensive force of National Guard and Police had taken advantage of the shallow embankment to establish a line of defence. Lightly armed with only MPT-9 machine guns, DshkM machine guns (similar to those mounted on the IC Toyotas) and Heckler light machine guns the Iranians attempted to hinder and with the help of God to halt the IC advance.

The railway embankment offered a considerable obstacle for the jihadist's armour to cross and impossible for the jeeps. Precious time could be gained for the defenders as Al-Malouf needed to calculate a strategy to breach the defence.

Faced with an impossible decision Akbari

finally had to concede defeat and accepted the terms offered by Pisinah. In his mind the President acknowledged that the future of his people was of a greater importance than that of his own.

With not a moment to loose President Pisinah summoned his small but select inner radical leadership, who had been anxiously waiting in the grounds of the Palace, to join him for an emergency war council in the Green Room.

Out in the main streets in the afternoon sun of Tehran the gathering of the public had swollen to well over two million occupying all the streets of Azadi, Enghelab, Vali Asr, Azarbayjan and Kaigar as well as the Laleh, Nasr and Pardisan Parks plus several main highways.

Wasting not a second the grey haired Pisinah arranged for a microphone and speakers to be hurriedly erected on the balcony of the Green Room. Holding the microphone to his mouth he spoke to the tumultuous rioting crowd below,

"My friends, my friends it is I Yadullah Pisinah. Akbari has been ousted and I am now your President" an immediate roar of approval rose from the crowd, *"The jihadist Sunni enemy is in the western suburbs of the*

city. The Guard and Police are in defence but their strength is limited. To save our beautiful city I want you all to rush to the area and overwhelm the invaders. Many hundreds if not thousands of you will die but this is the price we must pay. I am also going to order the Air Force to bomb the west suburb of Tehran. There is no other way. Now go and kill Al-Malouf and his jihadist terrorists. Kill them all. Go!!!"

The message rapidly spread amongst the gigantic crowd like a chant from heaven, all the way to the Azadi Tower.

After the initial euphoria subsided and the full reality of their situation sank home, a silence fell across the city, apart from the area around the railway line. This was soon broken however as one after another gunshot was placed skyward in support in Pisinah. The elderly dissident from Esfahan had succeeded in re-directing the intense anger of the entire crowd of two or so million people toward the utter destruction of the terrorist invaders, no matter what the cost.

Halted by the Iranian defence Al-Malouf with the assistance of Gajari had ordered fifty of the Toyota gun ships to advance, in five rows of ten abreast, along the A-Saidi Highway and obliterate anything in their

path!
Once the jeeps had climbed the shallow roadside bank and successfully lined up across both sides of the dual carriageway .. they started forward at a steady ten miles per hour.

Gajari had all his tanks and howitzers throwing whatever they could at the Iranian defence dug in on the far side of the railway. The pounding was terrifying, the stench of cordite was overwhelming and the dying was awful! The jeeps soon encountered their adversary and with the first row of ten Dshk 12.7mm machine guns releasing six hundred rounds a minute each soon obliterated the Police highway defence. But then came the time for the second row of Toyotas to replace the first and face the oncoming angry crowd spilling down to the junction of A-Saidi and Navab Safawi highways. The jeeps stopped for a moments thought.

Gajari ordered the tanks to advance into the railway cutting and cross the railway.

At this point the first wave of F-4's and F-14's appeared in the skies directly above Tehran. Based at Khatami-Esfahan and Shiraz just a few minutes flying time to the south the pilots reluctantly began to obey the orders from their new President and swooped down

to release bombs on the suburbs of south western Tehran. They were bombing their own capital city! and killing their own people in the process!

This took Al-Malouf by surprise not thinking that Akbari had the bottle to do this..he was not yet aware of the change in the Iranian leadership.

The scene in and around Vali-e Asr, Esmail Abad, Shad Abad and Khazaneh was apocalyptic .. the destruction immense. The now afternoon sun was shut out by the abundance of smoke and debris rising high above the city.

Pisinah could clearly see the multitude of columns of black putrid smoke and the thunder of so many explosions.

Another wave of five aircraft followed by a further two waves released their payloads onto the jihadist invaders.

Al-Malouf's losses were mounting to the point of worry. With the wide open space of the silent commercial airport of Mehr Abad lying just beyond the Iranian defence line on the north side of the embankment, Gajari pressed his advance up the cutting with all haste.

On seeing the pounding their brothers were

receiving from the air the jeep drivers now had no hesitation in moving forward along the dual carriageway towards the oncoming crowds.

The release of six hundred rounds per minute from ten 12.7mm DshK's into a solid wall of human beings was not a sight for the faint hearted!! The huge rounds tore threw the flesh, which offered no resistance and into several bodies behind. They fell to the ground like a tsunami wave of humans. Hundreds and hundreds of unarmed citizens of Tehran fell. As soon as the DshK magazines emptied the next row of jeeps took over and opened up into the crowd.

As the fifth and last row came forward their motion was halted by the sheer number of bodies in the road blocking the way. Even the crowd, so intent on reaching the jeeps to kill the occupants had great difficulty in climbing over the corpses to proceed forward. An impasse prevailed but still the row of Toyotas kept their guns blazing until the magazines could supply no more rounds. Their muzzles glowed with heat. Suddenly a shout came from a young man in the crowd,

"Down, get down" as he threw a grenade with as much force as he could muster to

cover the distance over the dead.

Boom! as it exploded throwing several corpses into the air.. Not far enough. He did not reach the jeeps. The extent of the bodies was too great for his throw to overcome!

Several of the tanks had finally managed to climb the bank amid the torrent of bombs from above and came face to face with the inadequate weaponry of the Guards and Police. The machine guns opened up and delivered a devastating wall of lead into the lines of the Iranian forces. They fell to the ground in their droves allowing the hundreds of jihadist foot soldiers to top the embankment and run across the airfield to the relative safety of the terminal building and various hangers on the far side. The armour followed churning up the flat grassy desert as they accelerated on full power. Parked on the concrete dispersal pad were two Iran Air jets, one large Boeing 747 jumbo and and one small Airbus 319. Sitting glinting in the sun they presented admirable targets for the forward tank crew commanded by Al-Malouf himself.

The first shell caught the jumbo just short of the midship door with the second taking out the huge tail section. The plane exploded sending millions of fragments of molten aluminium high into the air amidst the ball of flame. The second tank took the Airbus on it's nose sinking the aircraft unceremoniously into a bow as the nosewheel gave way. The terminal building took several shells before collapsing into a pile of steel and glass rubble. Still the air strikes from the Iranian F-14's and F-4's continued unabated successfully depleting the IC force with each wave of bombing. It was Captain Samadi in his twin engined Grumman F-14 Tomcat, having just dropped his five hundred pound payload, that caught the Syrian shoulder held RPG (Rocket Propelled Grenade) in his starboard wing forcing him to instantly eject from his doomed machine. His aircraft then entered a deep spin and dropped into the middle of the crowd close to the Azadi Tower. The impact explosion threw hundreds of the crowd skyward. The burning aviation fuel ran down the road igniting anyone who came into contact with it, burning them alive. The tower itself sustained considerable damage from the blast to the point of raining masses of white marble debris into the crowd further adding to the casualties. The scene around the once beautiful Azadi Monument was indescribable.

The carnage encouraged the tenacity of even more and more innocent citizens of Tehran, now in their hundreds of thousands, to plough their way toward the airport and suburbs of Esmail and Shad Abad to unleash their anger upon the terrorist invaders.

Back at the Azari/ A-Saidi junction where the massacre of so many unarmed men, women and even a fair number of children would sicken the hardest of men, a divine intervention would seemed to have prevailed as for no apparent reason the guns of the Toyota born jihadists suddenly fell silent!

The prospect of just mowing down row after row after row of unarmed citizens just seemed to be pointless but more importantly it was the sheer extent of the Iranian tenacity and will to defend their city that actually drew a salute of respect from the jihadists. The priority of reloading the gun magazines took second place to the gradual withdrawal of the Toyotas who, strangely, now deemed it more honourable to fight against armed soldiers. On hearing of this withdrawal

Al-Malouf was furious and immediately ordered the jeeps back into the frey until all their armoury of bullets had been fully exhausted! Confusion now sat with the Fifty

Toyota crews knowing that counter-manding their leader's orders would certainly lead to their own execution.

The justification of the cause for the rise and advancement of the Caliphate won them over. Back up the Highway they drove with magazines fully reloaded and guns cocked.

Having found that crawling over the river of corpses impeded progress too much, many of the Iranians had grabbed the front doors, floorboards and all flat wood from the shops and houses in the street to lay over the human road to form a new solid surface. It was not easy for the advancing crowd to tread over the dead with so much impunity and disregard but there would be time for praise and prayers when the day had been won.

Like a streak of lightning news of the massacre at Azari spread through the crowds and soon reached the ears of Pisinah residing in the safety of the Palace. The reported extent of the carnage ran deep even into the hardened people's leader from Esfahan, so much so that he ordered the commander of the F-14 Squadron at Shiraz to ready a couple of aircraft and undertake an immediate surgical strike on the road junction. As expected the commander pointed out the risk of many Iranian casualties in such a mission with their limited accuracy using these old fourth generation aircraft. Putting these risks to one side Pisinah, whilst acknowledging the possible outcome and accepting full personal responsibility, insisted on the order being carried out with the utmost of speed.

Gajari and his armoured division made good progress across the open airfield to join up with Al-Malouf taking refuge in one of the cargo hangers. The cost of breaching the railway and dashing crossing the open airfield had been high. On reviewing the scene through the hanger window Al-Malouf could clearly see at least half of his remaining armour smouldering in the putrid black inferno of Mehr-Abad airfield. In the heat and confusion of the engagement little did he or Gajari appreciate the advancing throng of Tehran's population down the Lashkari Expressway and Me'raj Blvd. They had broken through the perimeter fence of the airport and the wall of four hundred or so thousand were just a few hundred metres from the north side buildings which included the cargo hangers.

Chapter Twelve

Captain Piruz flew in from the south west reducing his F-14 Tomcat to five hundred feet with wings extended to thirty five degrees for a low speed approach using the control tower of Mehr-Abad Airport as his guide reference. Locking onto the top end of the A-Saidi motorway with his primitive bomb aiming computer he came in at two hundred knots. Through his cockpit glass Piruz could clearly make out the massacre scene ahead with the ground swelling with fellow Iranians advancing down the road. With his hand on the red release trigger and the target rapidly approaching Piruz hesitated for a couple of seconds with the sure thought of him killing hundreds of his own people. The two five hundred pounders dropped serenely from his wing impacting with the ground sixty metres forward of the Toyota line whilst he slammed both of his throttles forward engaging full afterburners to draw upon the almighty push of fifty six thousand pounds of thrust from the two General Electric F-110's and drew in his variable geometry wings for a high alpha climbout.

The simultaneous explosions sent chunks of tarmac and concrete hurtling into the Iranian crowd drawing anger towards the massive incompetence of the pilot. The second Fighter jet faired much better with his aim who planted his five hundred pounders within the IC group taking out many of the jeeps.

Still the crowd advanced. Like a human river the 'push' from those at the rear, who could not fully appreciate the carnage and misery being perpetrated at the head of the crowd, supplied an unstoppable momentum. What Toyotas that survived the second air strike were now fulfilled with renewed resolve to carry out their orders. Once more six Dshk's opened up impacting three thousand six hundred 12.7 mm rounds per minute into the oncoming human river.

Men, women and even several children fell to the Syrian lead as once more it tore through their bodies, but still they advanced!

On his second attack Captain Piruz was resolute to make amends for his previous attempt with the use of his Vulcan 20 mm cannon. Again with an airspeed of two hundred knots he emptied his full six second burst. A row of bullets ran up the dual carriageway to meet the IC jeeps taking out three. In came the second F-14 Tomcat who managed to eliminate two more. The drivers of the remaining four serviceable jeeps now realised that their position was hopeless and violating direct orders attempted to turn their Toyotas around and drive away from the ever encroaching crowd. There was not enough time. The crowd, having sensed the withdrawal of the enemy, crawled across their dead brothers and sisters with the utmost determination and vigour managing to reach the jeeps before they had completed their abouturn. The terrorists stood no chance of surviving the hate and revengeful fervour of the Iranian crowd. Each in turn was dragged from his vehicle and beaten and kicked to a pulp before several of the crowd picked up some debris from the road and smashed it down on the head of his victim. The heat of the moment got to one of the more elderly of the Iranian women as she pounded and pounded the face of the poor Syrian with a brick. Not a lot the the man's skeletal structure was left. Such was the vengeance demanded by the normally quiescent people of Tehran.

With this localised revengeful kill complete

and their adrenalin levels reducing back to normal, the forward placed members of the Iranian crowd took time to stand tall and look back at the scene of atrocity and contemplate the enormity of the price their fellow Shia Muslims had just paid. The pile of unarmed corpses stood six to seven feet high, stretching the full width of Azari Blvd right back for around one hundred metres. With difficulty it was estimated by several of those present that between five and six thousand lay perished in the road. The time for a respectful mourning would have to wait!

News of this small but extremely important victory sat well with Pisinah who immediately advised the Air Force to discontinue any further attacks in that area. The utilisation of the sheer power of a great number of people to overcome the force and brutality of the IC invaders now, in his eyes, gave Pisinah full justification for his initial order.

Brimming with confidence the man from Esfahan then issued further orders for the Air Force to deliver a battalion of armed troops behind the IC field of battle at Mehr Abad Airport and engage their rear. He could smell the sweet scent of success of victory in his nostrils.

The vast residue of the crowd from Azari junction, still knumb from the reality of the situation, could clearly hear the shelling and gunfire at the Airport not five hundred metres away, so to a person re-engaged their tenacity and desire for revenge headed along Shamshiri and Ghazvin Blvds toward the eastern fringes of the airport to support their fellow citizens of Tehran.

Sufficiently rested, rearmed and having consolidated his position with what was left of his leadership team whilst sheltering within the confines of the Iran Air maintenance hangers Al-Malouf felt ready to break out and continue his advance onto the new Parliament Building in Baharestan Square. This, in his infinite wisdom, he saw as the heart of the city and the one place from which he could exercise his full authority, once Tehran had been sacked.

The spearhead of this final push was heralded by the few T-72's which broke through the flimsy rear aluminium wall of the enormous hanger at which point the tank commanders saw the true reality of what was between them and their goal .... two million, mostly unarmed, civilians of Tehran. Having torn down hundreds and hundreds of metres of the reinforced steel perimeter fence the vast crowds were covering the few hundred remaining metres to the hangers, across the concrete, as fast as their legs could carry them only to be brought to a sudden halt at the sight of the Russian tanks as they broke through the wall the hanger wall.

"Fire. Fire with all you have!" ordered Gajari as he closed down his forward hatch and prepared to engage the innocent enemy.

Pow! Pow! as one after another the shells left the barrels of the IC armour. The remaining Toyota gunships screamed out behind the heavy armour with all Dshk's and KPV's on full chat. Behind them came the foot soldiers fanning out to take up a defensive firing line with their AK-47's.

All hell from Satan was being released upon the determined crowd as detonation after detonation ravaged carnage amongst the Iranian hoard. If ever there was an illegal massacre that would later require an appearance in the International Court in the Hague... **this was it!**

The four engined Lockheed C-130 with it's full complement of one hundred and twenty five fully armed paratroopers aboard circled unnoticed, high above the unfolding atrocity at Mehr-Abad Airport, whilst lowering it's rear ramp for the troops to jump from. On came the amber, then green light indicating permission for the paratroopers to jump. Out they went , two by two.

The heavy engagement against the advancing human river occupied the full attention of Al-Malouf and his thugs consequently never noticed the cloud of silk parachutes landing on the airfield grass far to their rear.

Gathering all his men together, having cut loose their silk sheets, Colonel Heydar issued the order for one hundred to rapidly advance in a single line abreast formation whilst the remaining twenty five dig in and set up their HM-12 medium range mortars.

In a short running style the Iranian commandos from Shiraz soon covered over half the distance between their landing zone and the IC rear line and could clearly see the action ahead. Time for the mortars to fly. Completely taken by surprise as the first of the mortars landed amongst them, confusion, confusion and more confusion began to set in within the jihadist army. With their Tondar sub-machine guns ready to shoot from the hip the commandos came to a halt, took aim and opened up on the continuous fire setting on their Tondars.

Many jihadists fell to the ground before abouturning and returning fire. Immediately the Iranians dropped to a lying down stance.

To the further surprise of the invading IC jihadists they caught sight of the second and then the third C-130 disgorging their payload of a further battalion of commandos.
Al-Malouf now felt that he was being closed in, so ordered his ground troops to return to the centre of the airfield and take on the airbourne commandos.
Despite the enormous casualties being sustained by the Iranian crowd the gulf between them and Tariq Gajari's tanks had diminished to just a few yards.
The strength and initial advantage of
Al-Malouf's position on entering Tehran, just a matter of a few hours previous, had suffered greatly to the point of virtually there being no hope of a victory. To his north was the huge oncoming crowd descending from Maraj and the Karaj Specific Highway, to his south east another oncoming crowd of large proportions from A-Saidi Highway and to his rear a build up of crack commandos. The IC force now found themselves totally surrounded.
Still the T-72's advanced but now they had

drawn so close to the Iranian masses that the tank barrels were too high to target the front line. Even the IC tank machine guns could not lower sufficiently to engage the Iranians. This allowed the many, including several of what was left of the police and National Guard, who had made it to this point, to be able to clamber aboard the advancing armour and tear down the menacing black pennants bearing the shahada inscription.

This was the turning point in the **battle of Tehran!**

With several hand grenades still at their disposal the Iranian National Guard, safely within the IC tank circle, strategically placed these grenades on the running track of each tank. Some were even lobbed into the tank and howitzer barrels following a discharge. As each grenade exploded the damage to the running gear of the T-72's was crippling bringing most of them to an unceremonious halt whilst others rotated in circles not being able to utilise one of their tracks for forward motion. The massive Iranian crowd was rapidly engulfing the Syrian armour.
To the rear of the IC stronghold the foot soldiers and remaining Toyota gunships were

heavily engaged in exchanging fire with the initial wave of commandos from Shiraz and were holding their own, however, as the second and third battalions completed their landing and started to join in the frey..the tables began to turn.

The sheer force of nearly five hundred fully armed professional Iranian commandos began to take charge of the secondary battlefield in the open grassland of Mehr-Abad Airport forcing the jihadists to pull back and face the baiting crowd which had now swamped the IC armour.

In the minds of the majority of the jihadist invaders the day was lost and could not see any way of escape. Al-Malouf himself, sat safely within the armoured confines of his T-72, took a similar disposition. The sheer overwhelming number of people, albeit unarmed for the most and the movement of the majority of his tanks incapacitated, there could be no possible way of escape. The humility of surrender was never to be an option. Fully realising that all his followers would carry the same strong belief he knew that they would fight to the last and die an 'honourable' death before the eyes of their adored Prophet.

In a similar stance to that of 'Custer's last stand' and with no orders required from their leader, the mixture of international jihadists celebrated their final moments on earth by killing as many Shia Iranians as they possibly could before being themselves savaged by the marauding crowd. No sympathy, regret or remorse was evident from the savage crowd as one by one the invading terrorists were overcome and battered or stabbed to death in a most undignified manner. Many of the notorious black bandanas were torn from the heads of the dead invaders and held high in the air in honour of their expensive victory.

Those, including, Al-Malouf and Tariq Gajari, still held prisoner in the confines of their reinforced Russian steel prisons were the last to have time to say their prayers. The cans of petrol were found in a store room in one of the hangers and passed across the crowd to those who had climbed atop the tanks. Once doused with the flammable liquid the crowd drew back from the armoured vehicles leaving them stranded on the grass like distant sentinels.. The identity of the Iranian who finally ignited the petrol trail would probably never be known as he had deliberately covered his head with a large scarf.

The final act to signify the conclusion of the Caliphate and it's Caliph was done in silence allowing the 'whooosh' of the lengthy petrol trail to be clearly heard by as many people as possible. The eventual ignition of the petrol soaked T-72s and howitzers was excessive resulting in several dramatic explosions as each fuel tank in turn caught alight burning alive all those sheltering inside.

In his final act of defiance Al-Malouf opened his top entry hatch, climbed out and stood tall holding his adopted black flag on the turret of his T-72 to address the words,

"May the wrath of Allah be cast upon your house and all Sh.." in Urdu. The flames leapt around him and all consumed his erect body before it fell to the ground in a flaming ball of fire.

The radical Pakistani greengrocer from Lahore who had travelled the middle-east to establish his religious belief was dead. The Caliphate he instigated now finished....

....or so everyone thought?

As the illumination from the residue of the destroyed Caliphate armoury died down in the fading sunlight the stunned and forlorn crowd could be seen to part a way for the entourage trying to reach the battle-zone. It was President Pisinah in his black Mercedes and armed escort desperately attempting to reach the final resting ground of the man that had caused such devastation and misery over the past months. Finally the Mercedes came to a slow and dignified halt and out stepped the elderly man from Esfahan dressed in his traditional grey gown and white turban.

Without a word passing his lips he sauntered up to and around the smouldering remains of Al-Malouf. Then having taken a moment of reflection spat a voluminous quantity of sputum onto the blackened mess.

Surveying the area he became acutely aware of the price the people of Tehran had paid for obeying his orders. Strewn across the major part of the airport were thousands and thousands of bodies, many in the black jihadi suits but most in everyday Iranian clothes ....soaked in blood.

A period of silence hung, like an invisible cloak, over the full extent of the airport and into the suburbs of the city in a communal feeling of remorse. Then the crying and wailing started, just by a few at first then by a few more and then many more and then almost the entire crowd!

The final scene that beheld Pisinah as he stood with his hands cupped and head bowed was nothing short of apocalyptic!

The gentle tears that portrayed his grief, he left for all to clearly see. This massacre was of his doing but the thought of the alternative should IC have been allowed to succeed in their utter extinction of the Shia, would have been all the more devastating. Pisinah took solace from that thought.

Gently raising his head from his long period of consideration, President Pisinah was faced with a lone figure in a torn black Burqa slowly walking towards him from the crowd line. The President's security stepped forward to hinder the person's approach. Without fuss or bother Pisinah raised his hands to counter their efforts,

"No, let her come to me. What she has to say will be of great importance" he spoke quietly.

The figure stopped just feet away from her leader and slowly dropped to her knees. In their respect and dignity for the courage shown by the young woman, the crowd fell silent whilst patiently awaiting her words.

Reminiscent of a Biblical scene of a bygone era the woman slowly opened her Burqa to reveal the small bloodied body of her dead young daughter. Holding Haleh towards her President she uttered few words in a soft voice,

"My name is Shahla Ushtra.
Why? .... Why? Please tell me why?"

Both she and the crowd waited patiently for the reply. Placing his hand upon Shahla's head Yadullah Pisinah replied in his best Farsi,

" You tell me. One day, but not today, a solution will be found to resolve our religious difference with the Sunni. I am sorry about your loss."

Stepping to one side he then addressed the crowd,

"This day must never be forgotten. Go and rebuild your lives. Tomorrow will be another day in the history of our great country, Iran."

He walked back to the Mercedes and drove away through the human road at a slow comfortable speed.

The crowd shifted forward and sympathetically embraced the kneeling Shahla. It was a woman's cry from the front row that suddenly shouted out in abuse for revenge which inspired others to similarly follow with louder, then louder voices. Their attention was turned to the Syrian and Iraqi corpses scattered around with emphasis on that of the smouldering Al-Malouf lying beside the tank.

"Find some rope or wire!" shouted a voice.

"Look inside one of the hangers!" replied another as the pitch of revengeful crys grew ever louder, spreading like wildfire around the complete city.

Within minutes four men had found their way to the centre of the action carrying a roll of heavy gauge wire. At this point the crowd went wild preparing the corpses for public hanging. The dragging of the bodies by their feet across the airport grass to the preparation area was exercised with no due care or attention shown toward the jihadists, at which point the three metre lengths of wire were tied off around their ankles.

It would not be for an hour or so before several private open backed vehicles would appear in the preparation area into which the corpses were piled high before being driven away to the designated public viewing areas. No one person could claim responsibility for what was about to happen. It was an unsaid understanding within the population of Tehran that the corpses of the terrorists should be a lesson to those who might also contemplate the overthrow of Iran.

By midnight the roads of Azadi Avenue, A-Saidi Expressway, Navab Safavi Highway, Yadegar-Emam Highway and Engbelab and it's famous Square were lined with the dead invaders hanging by their feet from the trees and lampposts: thousands of them.

The rest of that night and through the next four days the bodies of those Iranian citizens who so innocently fell were buried in a mass grave site hastily prepared on the vast empty space lying north of the Lashkari Exressway.

Eventually the news of the defeat of the IC army and images of the hanging corpses was relayed around the globe and to the many was received with relief ..

......but there was a minor element embedded deep within several countries that were
NOT!
Central Africa would soon strike the media headlines !

The Coalition that had sat helplessly at the Iranian border for the past days in Iraq were ordered to disband and return to their independent countries but it was the Council in Jerusalem that sat in conference burning the midnight oil!

With the relatively understanding Akbari now deposed and languishing in an open prison having been replaced with the 'known to be' more radical Cleric from Esfahan, would the consideration toward Israel now become more aggressive?

Did either country foresee an opportunity for a change in direction??

Jon Grainge's Tears in Tehran

Images
pertaining to this story for general consideration

———————

Rubble in street in Aleppo, Syria

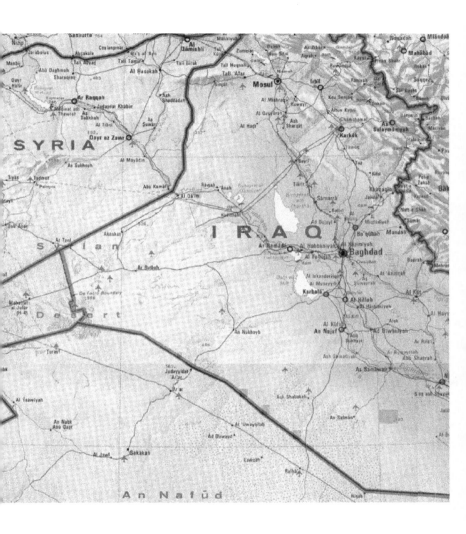

Map of Iraq and it's borders
with Syria and Iran

Map of Syria

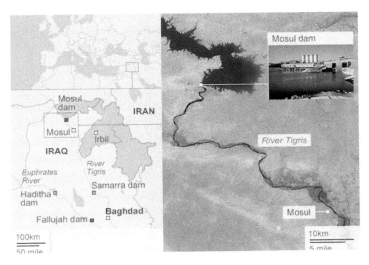

Course of River Tigress

Iranian F-4 Phantom

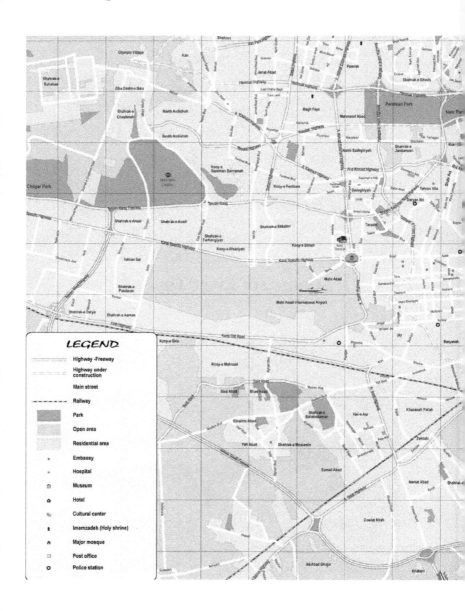

Layout of Tehran, Capital of Iran

Mosul Dam, Iraq

Azadi Tower, Tehran

Russian T-72 tank of the Syrian Army

Crowds leading to Azadi Tower, Tehran

Iranian Air Force F-4 Phantom

A. Saidi Highway near Mehr-Abad Airport

Tank shell explosion in Mosul, Iraq

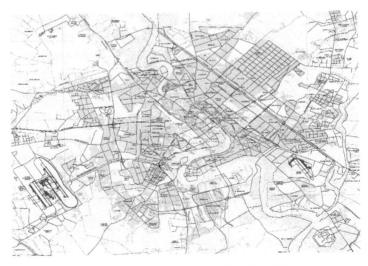

Map of Baghdad, capital of Iraq

Toyota gunships

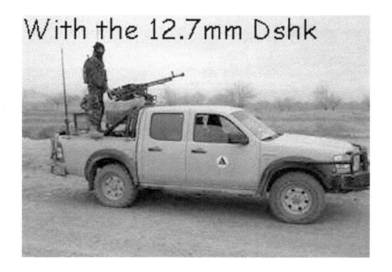

Lightning Source UK Ltd.
Milton Keynes UK
UKHW021928270519
343407UK00001B/6/P